AND THE LAUGHTER RANG ABOUT US—

"Something here wanted us, made this place for us. Now it doesn't want us anymore."

"Would we be better off in space, in the coffins?"

"Yes. We'll leave together and we'll be picked up or we'll die. At least it will be our choice, and not the command of some—some awful—"

We heard the laughing again, loud. We struck up the beach toward the coffins. There was a terrible rumbling behind us and the beach fell away into a rocky pit. We began to run, while around us the laughter grew. . . .

—*Case and the Dreamer*

More Science Fiction from SIGNET

Case
and the
Dreamer
and other stories

by
Theodore Sturgeon

A SIGNET BOOK
NEW AMERICAN LIBRARY
TIMES MIRROR

Acknowledgments
"Case and the Dreamer" appeared in *Galaxy*, January, 1972.
Copyright © Universal Publishing and Distributing Co.

"If All Men Were Brothers, Would You Let One Marry
Your Sister?" appeared in *Dangerous Visions*,
Copyright © 1967 by Harlan Ellison.

"When You Care, When You Love" appeared in
Fantasy & Science Fiction September, 1962.
Copyright © 1962 by Mercury Publications.

Contents

herself to herself, mostly, and took orders—not be_____this was a woman, because the Space services in_____and X? in particular required_____distinctions: actually_____were more female officers than men. Jan took orders_____se she was a rating and he was an officer ... to begin_____and after that began_____

CASE AND THE DREAMER

If, at the very moment Case died, someone had aimed a laser (a tight one, one of the highest intensity ever) at the spot from Earth, and if you could have ridden the beam-front for a thousand years (you couldn't, of course, and anyway, nobody aimed, nobody knew), you might have seen his coffin.

It wasn't meant to be a coffin. Ships have lifeboats when they fail, and the boats have lifebelts in case *they* fail, and the coffin had once answered that purpose; but now and for all those centuries, it was and had been Case's coffin.

It lay in lightlessness, its wide-spectrum shrieks of distress forever stilled. It tumbled ever so slowly, pressed long ago by light long gone, because it had never been told to stop.

Case, aged a thousand and some hundred and perhaps a couple of dozen and a fraction (but then, do the dead grow older?), lay in the sealed cylinder, dressed in inboard fatigues (which long ago—even in Case's long ago—had evolved into practically nothing) consisting of barely enough material to carry his brassard: Senior Grade Lieutenant, and the convoluted symbol of his service branch. EX^n, it read, once you got past the art: Ex-on many levels: exploration, extrasolar, extragalactic, extratemporal, and more; plus the possibility matrix: expatriate, ex-serviceman, ex-officio, exit . . . for on entering X^n, no man made plans for himself—not if they involved any "here," any "now." Or anyone . . .

An invisible, intangible something brushed the coffin, just once (for once was enough), and there then appeared something utterly outside Case's experience in all the exploration, all the discovery, all the adventure in his conscious life. It was a stroboscopic flicker which, more swiftly than the eye could comprehend or the brain register, became with each pulse a structure twice as large as it had been before, until it reached a point hardly ten meters away from the tumbling coffin, and stopped, glowing. There was no deceleration in this approach, for there was no motion as motion is understood. With each pulsation the craft—for it was indeed a ship—ceased to exist *here* and reappeared *there*. The distance between *here* and *there* was controllable and could vary widely; it must be so, for the approach (if it can be called an approach, in a vessel which in and of itself never moved) doubled its apparent size except for the last three pulses, during which its "approach" was meters, a meter, some centimeters.

A brief pause, then a disk no larger than a saucer spun out from the seamless hull of the vessel, hovered for a moment near the slowly tumbling coffin, then fell back and around to match its rotation. It placed itself near one end of the coffin and emitted a squirt of flame, and another. The tumbling slowed and, with a third impulse, stopped.

Another pause, while emanations from the ship probed, bathed, searched, touched, tested, checked, and rechecked. Then on the flawless hull appeared a pair of lines and another, transverse, making a rectangle. Inside the rectangle the hull appeared to dissolve. The tiny saucer moved behind the coffin and made its meticulous squirt, and the coffin moved precisely through the intersection of imaginary diagonals athwart the doorway.

Inside, four columns of pale orange light sprang upward from the deck, supporting and guiding the coffin until it was fully inside, whereupon the rectangular opening hazed over, darkened, became solid, seamless hull again. With a brief, shrill hiss, atmospheric pressure appeared, equalizing the outside of the coffin's shell with whatever was inside. Then the orange beams turned the coffin and moved it toward a spot on the forward bulkhead which irised open to a corridor, a tall oval in cross-section, glowing with sourceless, shadowless, pale blue-white light. Again a doorway shut behind the coffin, and it was moved smoothly and silently up the corridor, past a row of closed oval doors and shuttered ports, to an open door near the far forward end of the corridor. Here the beams checked the coffin, turned it, and slid it into a room. It came to rest in a space between two banks of equipment. On the left was apparently a control panel of some complex kind, though it carried no switches or knobs, but had instead arrays of small disks floating two handsbreaths away from the panels, each, when activated, glowing with its own hue and with intensity according to the degree of function. On the right was a great bank of indicators. Case (if he had been alive) would have found the calibrations and indicators incomprehensible.

There appeared on the walkway which now surrounded the coffin a blue man, hooded and gloved, whose body dazzled without being excessively bright, who seemed to be not quite transparent yet not solid; who seemed in some way out of focus. At no time did he touch anything with his small hands, and he moved without a stride—he seemed to glide or slide from place to place.

He stood for a time with his hands behind him and his hooded head bent, regarding the coffin, and then turned to the control bank. Deftly he activated a half-dozen systems by passing his hand between the face of the console and one after another of the floating disks, each of which lit up. A gate at the front of the room opened and two metal arms, bearing a semicircle of glowing bus, moved the length of the coffin, down and back. The field of the curved busbar rendered the top half of the coffin transparent. The arms retracted, the gate closed. The blue man made his swift, touchless passes at the console and the various glowing, floating disks faded to dark.

The blue man placed his hands behind his back and stood for a long time regarding the body inside the coffin—the (compared with his own) over-long arms and legs, the hint of bony ridges over the corpse's eyes, the heavy pectoral muscles and the flat stomach. After a time he glided around to the other side of the coffin and inspected that view, the hollow needles still embedded in the antecubitals, the bronze-colored, tonsure-shaped helmet clamped to the head, at the thick hair which tumbled around its edges, and for a long time astonished while at that phenomenon, once Case's shame and embarrassment, later his flag of defiance—his beard, which in the last days of his life he had allowed to grow far past the limits imposed by X^n.

The blue man returned to the controls and set up a complex sequence. Again the gate at the front of the room opened, and a new device trundled out and approached the coffin. It looked like a fair segment of a planetarium, a multiple projector studded with gimballed lenses and the housings of small and highly diverse field generators, together with a positioning frame and sets of folded, tool-bearing arms. The telescopic legs arched and straddled the coffin and positioned the projector over it. Urged by the sure, fleet hands of the blue man, the projector came alive with thread-like beams, some visible and brilliant, blue, gold, scarlet; some invisible but faintly shrill in the thin atmosphere which the room had assumed to match that inside the coffin. These beams were probes and stimulators, pressors and tractors, gauges and analyzers, samplers and matchers and testers.

Without pause, now, they reached their summations

and took further action. Mechanical hands searched and solved the seals. Gases were mixed and injected while the atmosphere in the chamber was matched in quality and kind and pressure (a process which had no effect whatever on the blue man) and then the seals were cracked, the coffin opened. While the body remained where it was, the opened coffin sank away to and through the deck. Case's corpse seemed to be floating in midair, which it was not, for although gravity had not yet been applied, it was held from drifting or shifting by the tractor beams, while the crouching machine tapped the tubes from the needles in Case's arms, severing them as the coffin dropped away, replacing their contents with something new. The same process was used on the small bronze helmet, all its leads analyzed, duplicated, tapped, and the original severed and discarded. A diathermic field adjusted the body's temperature, through and through, and all at once, tubed needles snaked out to the groin, the abdominal cavity, the sides of the neck. Warm fluids began coursing through them while pressor beams gently manipulated the joints, the muscles, the chest.

. . . and suddenly Case sat up, but you can't sit up afloat in midair supported by intangible columns of force and entangled by needle-pointed tubes, electrodes, probes. Even so, his movement was so sudden and so violent that the swift reflexes of the blue man, the built-in fail-safes of the systems, could not prevent his wild angry flailing and his tortured shout, *"Jan!"* But that was as far as he got before the massive tranquilizer hit his brain and he relaxed, sleeping.

Two tubes were gently replaced.

A broken hollow needle was extracted and another put in.

And a sleeping man is not a dead man. *Let him sleep,* said the master computer, and the blue man dissolved away and the lights dimmed, and Case slept.

"Jan!"

Tortured and hoarse, yes, but it has not been like the syllable that tore his throat and half his mind, mingled with the continuing crash of his chemical jets, abetted by the crush of acceleration, a multiple of anguish and loss and terror and love and fatigue (he hadn't known about the love before) on that terrible launch, the last before he died. There were the lifebelts, the coffins, side by side on the escarpment where he and Jan had dragged them, where they had tumbled in barely ahead of capture by the—by the—(a thought missing here: occluded, forgotten . . . ?) and—and—

And his craft was launched, and hers had not.

No one, not ever anywhere, no one has been so helpless, so furious. Programming in the escape belts was so simple it was implacable; he himself had set up the sequences, he himself had taken the irrevocable precaution of locking them in, of tying his command controls to hers, of canceling any possible override. And—

And his craft had launched, and hers had not, had not, had not.

Jan!

Case slept on in the dimness, apparently free-floating, actually caged by gentle, unbreakable beams. After enough hours (the master computer knew exactly the meaning of "enough"), the sourceless light increased, and with it, the figure of the blue man appeared and gained its almost-density. Moving to the console, the blue man activated certain of the telltales on the opposite bulkhead and studied them. Apparently satisfied, he turned back, made a number of careful adjustments, and then passed his hand behind a master-switch disk.

Immediately a deep hum began, grew in intensity until checked by the blue man's intangible hand, and then began to rise in pitch, fall again, rise and steady. It began **to** pulsate: eleven, fourteen, sixteen cycles . . . eighteen . . . and there it held. Then began a series of matching tones, high harmonics, multiples, tones set apart by fractions to set up beat frequencies; these in turn orchestrated to the heavy subsonics, the entire structure of sound constantly self-adjusting to itself and to the readouts connected through Case's bronze helmet, until at last the whole living sonority was tailored exactly to him, to the emanations of his brain, the doorways of his mind, the subtle temporal cells, the neurons and synapses of his brain.

Case was no longer asleep.

This was something far deeper.

Something began to press against the integument of his mind, gently, irresistibly, until it dissolved the wall and entered. It sought out those storage cells as yet unoccupied, meticulously respecting treasures and privacies, looking into nothing, asking only space to lay down new learning. Once this was found, it withdrew, leaving (remember: all is figure) a line into each compartment

Now there swiftly flowed through these lines new knowledge and new ideation. Language. Idiom. The ideological, analogical, mythological underbracing of idiom. Case was given everything a colleague and contemporary of the blue man might be expected to have, except knowledge of himself and his current situation. That he would get in his own way, in his own time: the ultimate courtesy.

The hypnotic sound faded. The lights changed slightly. The blue man put his hands behind his back and waited.

Case awoke.

There is no end to the wonders of the universe, and no acrobatics of the imagination through time and space are needed to find them. A twentieth-century man could, if he would, spend half a lifetime in learning all there is to be learned about a square foot of topsoil, six inches deep. He would find animals and insects with marvelous abilities, able to speak languages of scent as well as sound; whole generations of aggression and defense; funguses capable of weaving nooses quick and strong enough to snap around a salamander, ingenious enough then to wrap and digest it. On the microphysical level are the endlessly subtle phenomena of solution and suspension, of freeze and thaw, while the living things encapsulate and encyst and metamorphose . . . no end of wonders.

Consider then the cattle tick. Hatching in the ground, she sheds and grows and sheds and grows some more, and sheds and mates. At last, carrying within her the encapsulated sperm, she climbs. Eyeless, she is yet guided to climb upward until she finds a limb-tip where she clings until her reflexes are fired by a single, special spark: the odor of butyric acid, which is found in the sweat of warm-blooded mammals. At that, she leaps and, if she misses, will climb patiently again and find another tip, and hang there waiting. She has been known to hang there for *eighteen years*—and yet will react instantly and fully in the presence of the one thing she is equipped to take and designed to need. She will feed for a day, whereupon she releases the sperm she has hoarded to the eggs she carries. She falls then and dies, and the fertilized eggs are ready to take up the cycle.

Her life, then, is composed of instants and episodes (as is yours) and could you communicate with her, she might recall episodes: the second shedding, the mating, the climb, the leap. the wait, through drought, freeze, drench, windstorm—why, that was another instant, another moment, for during that time she could be called alive only by nearly misusing the word; it was another instant, and less memorable than that first plunge into warm blood.

Case's first awakening, then, was but an instant after that terrible launch (for he could, but would not remember the long despair during which he gave himself to the belt's life-support, life-suspension systems). He might have forgone these through grief and fury had not his own emergency programming been as implacable and unforgiving as that he had laid on to the belts, unconscious, automatic, indelible.

(But hers didn't launch, didn't launch.)

Therefore Case awoke (the first time) but an instant after that terrible wrench; therefore his hoarse cry; therefore he was the only human being in all the universe who could remember so distant an event as the escape from that hellish unknown planet; and to him it was not distant at all. For such is the nature of time, that a man's clock and a man's soul might give him true measurements, but the truth need not be the same. If you are to understand Case, you must understand this.

So it was that he knew time had passed when he awoke the second time; he knew he had been asleep. He knew he felt well and rested, and that he was hungry and thirsty. He did not know where he was, and when he tried to sit up he could not.

"Lie still," said the blue man. "Don't try to move while I get those needles out of you."

Case's first disobedient reflex was to move, fast and hard. When he again found he coudn't, he saw the sense of it and relaxed. The blue man made quick, sure passes at the console, and a piece of equipment glided out of the bulkhead somewhere beyond his head, came to him, extended glittering gentle arms and tools and drew the tubes, applied cool creams, released, untied, removed the various devices which had given him back his life (and all trace that they had ever been there) while he lay wondering what language the blue man had spoken—and how it was that he could understand it.

The equipment slid away from him and traveled to its gate in the forward bulkhead, which swallowed it. Case lay still, looking up at the blue man, whose hooded, concealed face could tell him nothing, but whose relaxed, hands-behind-back pose was one of watchful waiting. Mysterious, yes. Menacing, no.

Case moved tentatively, found no restraints, sat up. He sat on nothing visible and, looking down, found himself apparently afloat a meter above the deck. He had a second of vertigo, which passed as the blue man, with instant understanding, waved at a control. Case was immediately supported and surrounded by the soft, firm chair which faded in around him. He sat up straight, looked at the arms, around at the back, and then at the blue man, whose calming gesture was commanding enough to cause him to lean back—watchful of course, but no longer alarmed.

"Lieutenant Hardin . . ."

Case blinked. It was so long, even as he knew time, since he had heard that name that he had all but forgotten it was his. It was a little like being called by one's middle name, never having used it publicly before. "I'm usually called Case," he said. "And who are you?"

A pause, then the blue man (faceless, but with a smile in his voice) said, "There really is no simple answer to that question. For the time being, just call me the Doctor."

"Doctor." The word meant the right thing as he said it, but felt unfamiliar to his tongue and throat. "Doctor," he said again in his own (old) language. That felt better but he could sense it meant nothing to the blue man.

"That's right," said the Doctor, "you've learned a new language—new to you, very ancient to me."

The idea of hypnogogia—sleep-learning—was not unfamiliar to Case, though he had never experienced anything as—well, *finished* as this. Learning and using information by hypnogogia had always been an instant translation (or rapid analog) process to him: think "cat" and come out with "gleep," or whatever the appropriate word was in the learned system. In this case, he was *thinking* in the new language. Yet if he wished to use his old one, he could merely by decision, and without special effort. All gain, no loss.

Case closed his eyes. Did his new language have words for grief and anger and self-detestation? Yes, it had. Gratitude? *Saved my life . . .* There is this about dying anguished: that the anguish dies with you, and the pain. What then if you are revived, and with you, the anguish? This is what mattered at the moment, not a stupid "Where am I?" He was on a ship, which had picked him up. Whose ship, bound for where? That mattered too, but— not yet. Gratitude . . . ?

There were a million questions to ask, and nine hundred thousand of them conflicted with his conditioning: to give no information unless he must, and on certain matters, no information at all.

"You were the executive officer on the X^n ship *Outbound*," said the Doctor, "an Explorer class discovery vessel launched from Terra Central on a mission to penetrate the galactic arm and make certain experiments in intragalactic space, among them being to test a new version of the flicker-field mode of faster-than-light travel. A design error caused the vessel to accelerate out of control to velocities exceeding anything regarded at the time as theoretically possible. Compounding the *Outbound* disaster was the ship's ability to gather intergalactic hydrogen molecules for fuel, which, at the unexpected velocities, caused an increment exceeding expenditure of fuel. The only possible result must have been an explosion or other disruption of the vessel. What actually happened is not known, because by the time it happened the ship was far outside any possibility of detection."

Case felt a flash of irritation. "If you've picked all this out of my head already, why go over it?"

Gently the Doctor said, "We took nothing from you, Case. We respect personal integrity above all other things, and the privacy of a man's choices are his own. No: what I have just said came from the archives."

Archives. Not files or retrieval banks—archives.

"How long were we—was the *Outbound* lost?"

"By Terra Central reckoning—some twelve hundred years."

"I couldn't have been suspended for twelve hundred years!"

"You weren't. You died."

After a time the Doctor said, "Would you like to be by yourself?"

"If you don't mind," Case whispered.

The blue man faded and disappeared. Case saw this, but could only stare dully.

Jan. Oh, Jan. . . .

His mind then for a while was a wordless throb. Deep in his mind, where lives the observer all of us carry—the merciless one who stands off watching—was name-calling: *Idiot! Sentimental slob! Why is it a greater grief to you to know she is a thousand years dead than a mere two hundred? And Angry, are you? Angry! What are you going to do with your anger?*

"Something," he whispered. "Something . . ."

He flicked a slitted glance around. There was nothing in this bland place to strike out against, so with one blow he fisted his palm so hard he numbed it; and while waiting for it to begin to ache, he saw in memory a flash of ugly laughter. It was laughter all but standing alone, mouthless, deep, cheerful—the cheerfulness of a man with a better mousetrap, and Case (and Jan, and Jan) the mice. Why couldn't he remember the mouth, the face, the situation? For he *saw* this laugh in memory, he did not hear it.

Occlusion—the profound will not to remember. Occlusion is an act of survival, an unwillingness to replay some terrible shock. Yet occluded matter always leaves

a trigger in plain sight (here, a visible laugh) and that is
also a survival trait; for the deep mind wants always to
know where the danger is, and what to fear. To be as
close to his deep mind as Case was (his training had made
him so) was to tread always the edge of internal terrors,
to be placed always at the point of decision: shall I recall
the trauma? or bury the trigger again?—for only at
this edge did he have the ability to react with the fabled
swiftness of the X^n Corps.

He let the trigger, the laugh, fade and closed his eyes,
commanding some alternative to come to mind. Anything.
Anything else, anything instead. Something, perhaps, before the laughter.

Something like: before the laughter was the chase, and
before that the landing, and before that the lifeboat, and
before that . . . before that no one would ever know,
because they had abandoned ship in the flickering grayness
of translight velocity, under or over, who knew? There
was no instrumentation for that, and no instruments told
the truth anyway; electrons flowed in strange ways, coils
and fields were distorted and wild. No one had ever been
there before, no probe had ever reported back. Scuttlebutt,
off-duty talk: what would happen to you if you bailed out
of a ship at faster-than-light velocities? They said, as
you reach it, time approaches zero and mass approaches
infinity. Achilles and the tortoise; as logic approaches per-
fection, truth approaches zero. Someone said C (the terminal velocity) was a gateway into another universe, or
another phase in phased space. Some said, death and dis-
solution, for all the electrical phenomena of biochemistry
would, with all the rules of physics, be so changed that
organization of matter and of life would be disrupted. And
some said no: transformation phenomena (mass into
energy into space into time, each proportionately inter-
changeable) might retain *pattern,* and some inconceivably
different form of life might be possible. Over it all was

the certainty that to bail out, away from the guarding life-support, artificial gravity, and all the other tissues of the man-made womb that was a spaceship, would be expulsion into something utterly strange and hostile. Bailing out in the stratosphere, with 95 percent of the atmosphere underneath one, and a temperature drop of perhaps two hundred degrees . . . the name of that is Lethal. Multiply it by what, then, in space, in that strange country where time itself might turn on its tail?

And always the other argument: that velocity itself is not a commanding factor; that early in the days of railroading wise men said that the ears would bleed, the sight would fail, the blood be unable to circulate at twenty miles an hour; and that all the talk of C was the same logical untruth; speed has no absolute, velocity is always relative, and that the only danger in bailing out is the matter of being a hell of a way from anywhere.

Well, Case had found out (with Jan, with Jan) by doing it, and it hadn't taught him a thing, except maybe that one can live through it. Not how, not what happened to them. The shrill alarm, the echoing-everywhere voice saying *abandon*, the clutch of fear on the way to his assigned lifeboat station when the mail hull started to buckle and the airtight barrier slammed down between him and his boat (and a good thing too; that whole section of the ship cracked away and exploded outward, boats and all) and the lights gone, the gravity gone, the wild scramble through familiar-unfamiliar gates and corridors to his alternate station, where he tumbled through the hatch (on top of someone else, he didn't know who) and kicked out and squirmed around, treading the other as he craned back to the corridor to see if anyone else was coming; but then, you couldn't *see*. If there was or was not, his conscience was clear (though his regret could never be) for the automatic override canceled his manual launch controls and he fell back into the lifeboat as it clanged shut and banged away from the ship. The boat's inertia-field took over at launch and saved them the terrible agony of acceleration, but its vibratory effect, chiming down the scale, was an agony of its own. His shipmate was as preoccupied with this as he, and the only thing he could clearly recall was a spinning glimpse of the ship with a ragged cavity in its midsection— the first part to blow off, the part that had contained his lifeboat station—limned in flickering arcs as the ruptured power cables lashed and vomited.

Probably they were both unconscious for a time. Case remembered a hazy inspection of the instruments, which had no useful information for him at all, except that the craft was sound and that its converter was picking up a reasonable amount of usable atomic hydrogen, so that fuel and life-support would not be a problem. Almost detach- edly he watched his hands on the controls, running through the implanted checklist, setting the computer to hunt for a ship and/or a terrestrial planet, the drive to maximum (the computer would not use maximum, but in that set- ting, max. was available), and the life-support complex: on, with alarms. A touch on one control took inventory of all stores and reported them complete. Another applied spin. The lifeboat had the contours of a shark with an exaggerated dorsal fin. The body contained stores, convert- ers, fuel; the fin was instrumentation and living quarters for six. Spin was on the long axis; subjective "down" was therefore in the tip of the fin.

All snug, all safe.

No hope.

Plenty of room, plenty of food and air for six. With two, it was palatial.

He looked at last at the other one—not that he hadn't cared before, but because his ingrained priorities were condition first, personnel second.

His first reaction had to do with all the people it wasn't. It wasn't Old Growl, the captain, or that funny little Henny from the black gang, or Bowker, who had always puzzled him and whom he'd always wanted to know better when he could get around to it, or Mary Dee, who had never found out that he had liked her better walking away, such was her hair, such was her face. This was one of the background faces, one of the others, you know, the people that make up the bulk of the roster in your memory of one or another school you went to once. Gander, Dancer, something like that. Janssen. XBC, xenobiochemist, usually found in a corner with two or three others from Science Section, talking shop. Correction. Listening to other people talking shop.

"Janifer?"

"Janocek." She sat with an elbow hooked around a soft stanchion, where she had anchored herself before spin. She had apparently been watching the checkout intently, following it step by step. Case outranked her; the conditioning would defer to him but make her miss nothing of the routine. Clearly, at this moment they both felt the weight of the programming leave them. Optimum conditioning takes care of essentials—down to the finest detail, true—but then it stops. They were on their own.

"Case Hardin, Lieutenant S.G.," he said.

"Yes, sir, I know." There was a foolish pause. He should have known she knew. There were more ratings than officers on a ship. To the ratings, the officers were never a, well, sea of faces. And his "S.G." hung pompously in the air between them. Her eyes were long almonds, so bright they were opaque (but, one realized, not from the inside), and her hair was drawn back almost painfully tight from a seamless brow. She was slender, tall (both just this side of "too"), and there was an odd, controlled quality in her voice, as if it were kept in the middle register by a conscious effort. She asked, "What happened?"

He shrugged and nodded at the telltales. No ship, no

boats, no planet, no sun anywhere. Some debris, dwindling as their launch took them away; nothing large enough to have saved or sheltered anyone, else the computer would have it reported. As they spun, a paleness washed across the screens: the end of the arm of a distant galaxy. Case touched a control and fixed a view of it. "Nobody tells the ratings anything," she observed.

"They don't tell a lieutenant much, either. We were testing a new drive. Theoretically it wouldn't work in gravitic fields of a certain density, so we headed for deep space with a conventional drive. By the numbers, we were okay; the math section gave us a factor of safety of three or better; I mean, we were three times as far into inter-galactic space as we needed to be safe. Well—they were wrong, or the design was wrong, or they did something wrong on the bridge. They cut in the new drive, and couldn't turn it off. Nothing could turn it off. It was working outside our power supply, beyond control. We just accelerated until we broke up."

"And there's no one—"

"No one."

They found themselves looking at one another. What was happening behind the shine of those long eyes? *Why you?* Or was she mourning someone? For a second he had a deep flash of regret; he did not gossip, he did not pry, he never watched other people's affections and partnerings and personal peccadillos. Case had a searching and hungry mind, but it was pointed at the job, the responsibility, the mission; a deliberate repression of his own wants and an earnest subjugation to those of his superiors, and theirs. He was a good officer. Whether or not he was known as a good man had never concerned him. And ... perhaps it need not concern him now. He was half the population, and the ranking half at that. There wasn't anyone else for her to set standards and comparisons by, and from the looks of things, there wouldn't be. He sighed (why?) and

turned away from her. He had nothing to recollect about
her. He would have to start knowing her from scratch,
from this point forward, while she . . . well, she knew who
he was. In his world, one was used to living in close quarters with other people—there were so many of them,
everywhere. But because there were so many, there was
always a choice. But now . . .

He turned to the console, latched out the saddle and
sat down. He stared glumly at the faint stain of stardust
that was a galaxy—who knew which one—and the blackness everywhere else—and hopelessly set up the computation for its distance. Eight hundred light-years, nine?
Something like that, surely. The boat could accelerate to a
fraction of C—a large fraction, to be sure, but still a
fraction—and the suspension gear might keep them alive
for a minimum of two, a maximum five hundred years.

Of course, the boat was equipped to care for six; but
could the life-suspension systems be manifolded, so that
they could revive and use new gear before the old ones
were played out? Would the unused systems be effective
after that length of time?

He glanced over his shoulder. His biochemist might
have some answers. But first—some numbers.

Expertly he flicked the computer commands, demanding the range and distance of the nearest planetary body.
In scanning a galactic cloud, even at eight hundred light-
years, the computer could only operate in an area of
probability—to lay in a course to a point in the cloud
where terrestrial planets were most likely to be, and terrestrial planets are not *likely* to be anywhere. He set the
computer to seeking, and turned away from it. He had at
last done everything he could, and he hated that, dreaded
it. There was now nothing left but to face the whole
matrix of things he had never concerned himself with nor
trained himself for; for which no conditioning had ever
been offered him and for which a single word—infra-

rational—had been a big enough discard bag for him. He was trained to confront problems, not people, not a person, not, for that matter, himself. He turned to confront it, her, himself, and she was crying, and she said, "We're going to die, aren't we?"

Everything about her, body and voice and eyes, asked only a simple answer, a denial, and he didn't have it for her. He never thought of lying (that's for those who knew more about people than he knew) and it never occurred to him to touch her, which would have served quite well, for she could have made her own interpretation. He said, "I guess so, Janifer," and even got her name wrong.

"Doctor."

The sourceless light increasd and the blue man appeared. "I'm hungry," Case said.

"In the chair," said the Doctor. "Are you feeling better?"

Case knew what the Doctor knew from the wide array of telltales, and that it was not his physical condition that was the subject of the query. But "better"?

He said, "After the ship broke up I escaped in a lifeboat with a rating, a Janet Janocek, xenomicrobiologist." The wide soft arm of the chair slitted open and uncovered a one-liter warm sucker. Like the wheel and the needle, the sucker's design is impervious to centuries. He pulled strongly at it and swallowed. It was bland (he could understand this; tastes do change, and the whole posture of his—captor?—host? was to present, not to enforce) but satisfying. He eyed it and had another pull. He said, "I can't remember what happened after we realized we were beyond help, out of range, with no reason to hope."

"You were picked up in a 'belt—you called it a coffin. What happened to the lifeboat?"

"Oh, that was smashed up on the landing."

The Doctor did not comment, but waited. Case said,

"I mean, I can't remember what we did all those days, a hundred and four of them . . ." What he meant was that he wanted to remember them in order, every hour and minute, because now they were precious, priceless, and because now he could not understand why, except for certain vivid scenes, they were at the time a succession of gray on grays to be lived through. Because this was *Jan* he was with, *Jan*. Whatever she was later, she did not become: she *was* that, was when he watched her cry that once, sat watching her with his useless hands pressed between his knees, miserably, watching her cry until she stopped. Then the days . . . ship's time said they were days; and you can sleep just so much and spend so much time in the tingler (had she used everything in the tingler? He had. Oh, Jan!) and then you check the console and enter "Ditto" in the log, and then there's nothing else to do but confront the other person and you just don't know how!

And all the while, he thought with a kind of awe, this was Jan. Thus it is when anguish and grief loop back on themselves. He wished he had it to do over, terror and hopelessness and all; a small price for those hundred and four days, now that he knew who she was. Had been.

"I remember," said Case, almost smiling, "Jan's starting a discussion with me about living, about staying alive— about *why*. Why did we keep a log and check the console and do the active and passive exercises and the tingler and all—why, when we knew we were going to die? And all I could say was, what's changed? What's the difference, really, between what we were doing and what we had always done? We knew where we were going to die—right in that lifeboat, when the time came, but otherwise we were just like everyone else, everywhere, trying to stay alive as long as possible. I knew she hadn't wanted to die a hundred days ago and I knew she didn't want to die this minute, and neither did I. But why now? She demanded an answer to that; it was just something she didn't know.

And I said I didn't know either, but that everyone ever born has been under a death sentence just for having been born, and the fact that for us there was no hope did not change anything; hope makes life easier but it does not make life impossible; millions upon millions have lived long lives without it. And this discussion was on the hundred and second day, and the hooter started up." And at last Case did smile.

"The hooter."

"Collision alarm, condition yellow. Somehow out there we were coming up on something, or something was coming up on us. It was enormous, it shouldn't have appeared as it did, so close and without previous warning, but it did, and don't ask me for explanations.

"It was a planet, larger than Luna and almost as large as Terra. I shouldn't have said 'planet' because there was no primary, but you'll understand why I call it that.

"I thought Jan would cry again. Maybe she did. I was busy at the console.

"I probed for atmosphere—the object was big enough. Negative. I got it on the screen, and read the range, and I couldn't believe it. To appear so quickly, it had to be approaching from ahead, adding velocities . . . and even then, it should have been detected days before. But it wasn't ahead, it was angling in from the left. I computed the angle; it was only two hundred and fifty thousand kilometers away and intersection was a little over thirty hours. I got magnification on the screen . . . a rocky spheroid, but by radar alone I couldn't tell much more than that."

(And Jan had said, "Please . . . oh, please. . . ." and when he turned to look at her she was standing with her hands over her ears: "Please turn off the hooter, Case.")

Case did not explain to the Doctor why he had smiled again. "I needed light to make any kind of survey, but out there there was nothing, not even starlight. I remember thinking again that anything that size would have to have some sort of atmosphere, if only hydrogen falling in or orbital dust, so I probed again and got a positive."

"Your instruments—" said the Doctor.

"My instruments were wrong," interrupted Case, "or I used them wrong, or a lot of things happened I can't explain. All I can do is to tell you what happened."

Detecting Case's irritation, the Doctor raised small, shimmering hands. "Please."

"Or what I remember," mumbled Case. "Maybe they're not the same thing. . . ."

He took another pull on the sucker and swallowed and said: "I set up the spectros for analysis and that's one thing I won't ever forget—the readout for Earth Normal. It said 0.9, and then it waited and threw in another nine, and after a bit three more: 0.99999. That's mean temperature and pressure as well as composition, and I doubt Terra itself would give you a reading like that. And there's something about the way those nines came up that's important, that I can't quite get my hand on . . . I don't know." He shifted, picked up the sucker, put it down again. "I got some sleep then, six hours, leaving Jan on watch with orders to wake me and take her six. We didn't know what we were in for and we wanted to be rested.

"When she woke me we had light. The planet, planetoid, whatever, it had light. It looked like those old photographs of Venus, when she was first observed, before the cloud-cover was dispersed. The radar pix were the same as before, nearer now, but the opticals showed unbroken clouds. The velocities were so nearly matched that I could trust the iron mike to hang an orbit. I left a running check on the nature of that light. It was white, more or less—a mix; it came from the clouds.

"We slid into orbit nice as you please, and dropped in close enough so the spin was an embarrassment. I set the boat into a tail-in attitude with the big fin leading, and a steady One-G deceleration, which made it comfortable for us and easier on the sensors.

"You can't expect full and sophisticated instrumentation and controls on a lifeboat, but what we had was good and I used it to the limit. We had all the time we needed and the velocities were so well matched that the transition from orbital to controlled flight situations was made as gently and pleasantly as any textbook tour-boat ever did. I lost the red-alert feeling, canceled the six-on, six-off watches, and spent most of my waking time on the scans. Jan said she would make a report about the way I handled it."

(Jan watched everything he did—well, of course, it was such a change from those other weeks; and she jumped to do anything he asked her for; and one day she said suddenly, "Case, you're wonderful, you know that? And nobody knows but me. I've got to tell them, somehow I've got to tell them." This disturbed him far more than any unbelievable planetoid, and he had nodded to her and turned back to his console, glad he had something else to fix on. After that she spent a lot of her off-watch time murmuring into a voicewriter.)

"I set a spiral so gradual and so matched to the atmosphere densities that frictional heating was not a problem, only useful. We braked with it, we used the heat for hydrogen treatment; actually, I do believe we landed with full tanks because of that, not that it did us any good. . . . We reoriented, nose parallel and hung on the horizon, fin up and the living quarters gimballed over so that for us and the boat there was up and down again. We circled the planetoid in the high stratosphere—or what would be a stratosphere on Terra—and mapped.

"Once into the cloud cover we found that it was just that—a cover. The air underneath was clear, with occasional drifting cumulus; the weirdest thing of all, though, was that, from the underside, the cover was illuminated only on one half. I mean, imagine a hollow sphere, half black and half white, and call the white the illuminated part. The planetoid is inside this sphere, and the sphere rotates around it, so that even without a primary, the surface has day-and-night phases.

"I picked a number of likely spots and finally selected one. It was a long, narrow, sandy plain, like a beach, at the edge of a large lake, with forest—oh yes, there was vegetation—on the other side. It seemed fairly level and we could land on it with a clear run to get off again. I ran a full check on the manuals and then took over. I made fourteen, fifteen trial approaches before I lowered the gear and went in.

"You have to understand, the lifeboat was no kind of airfoil. She came in on what we called stilts—supporting jets—and maintained attitude with gyros. I was practically sitting on the stilts at ten meters altitude, and I had forward velocity down to about fifteen meters per second. A crawl. And then there was this terrible noise and we fell over sideways."

(A tearing scream, edged, stabbing, and Jan's screaming with it, and—and his too, he screamed: to be falling, to know in that split second that the boat was gone, that hope, born again, was gone again; and as they toppled, that other sound, that other terrible sound that made them scream again when terror overrode despair. . . .)

"It was a small lifeboat, but small is . . ." He spread his hands. "There were tons of it all the same, and it fell over and I could hear the hull plates crumpling and turning back. I think the two left-side stilts, fore and aft, cut out, and the two right ones added to the topple and she lay over on her side and slid and ruined herself. And when the fin levered over and hit the sand we were thrown so hard we hit the bulkhead, restraints and all—they pulled right out, they were never built for such a lurch from the side as that.

"It was night, that crazy kind of night, when I came out of it. I was lying on the sand with my head on Jan's lap and she was wiping my face with something cold."

(And breathing used-up little *hics*, dry catches at the long, far end of weeping. She'd been thrown clear, right out through a rapture in the fin, and in time had found him dangling against the outside of the boat by his restraints, with his blood painting down the bent plates. She had got him down somehow and then had gone off to the beach with a bit of foam insulation which she dipped in the water and brought back. When he got his wits about him he gave her hell for maybe inoculating him with God-knows-what from alien water. Her response, astonishingly, was to fall instantly asleep.)

"I hurt all down my life side, especially the skull and my hip, both scraped badly and bruised. Jan was shaken up and for a while, two days or so, I was afraid of internal injuries because she vomited a lot and moaned in her sleep. Then I guess we both got sick for a while, a fever and blurred vision; it is asking a lot of the biosystem to be thrust unprotected into an alien environment, even a kindly one."

(Kindly. Cool at night, warm in the daytime, clean air, on the high side of oxygenation. Potable water. It could have been worse—if that had been all there was to it. When there was more to it, it was worse.)

"It was at the end of the third day, as nearly as I can recall, that we shook off the sickness and were able to take a good look at the situation. We were bruised and hungry, but we were out of shock. Jan told me she had been having dreams—a dream, I should say, vivid and recurrent: a device like hands, sorting and shuffling cards, laying them out, gathering them up, shuffling and laying them out again, and she was the pack of cards. I would not mention that or even remember it if she hadn't described it so forcefully and so often. I had my own, too;

but then, fever, you know—" He made a wiping-away gesture.

"What were the dreams, Case?" asked the Doctor, and quickly added, "if you don't mind—" because Case dropped the sucker, clamped his hands together, frowned down into them.

"I don't mind . . . although it's not very clear any more; I tried too hard for too long not to remember, I guess." He paused, then: "Hard to grasp, and any words I use are like approximations, but . . . I seemed to be suspended from some kind of filament. One end was inside me, somehow, and the other was high up, in shadows. Circling around me were eyes. Not pairs of eyes or one pair, but— I forget the arrangement. And I realized that the eyes weren't circling me, but whatever held the filament up there was twirling it while the eyes watched, and then there was—"

"Yes?" The prompting was very gentle.

"Laughing," said Case, and he whispered, "Laughing." He looked up at the Doctor. "Did I tell you about that noise just before we crashed?"

"You mentioned a noise."

"Partly it was the gyro bearings," said Case. "I found that out later, after the hull broke up and I had a chance to look at the drive sector. You had to see that to believe it. The only way I can describe it is to ask you to imagine all the bearing assemblies—every one of them, mind you— while turning at max, instantaneously turned solid, welded into one piece. The shafts had wrung big ragged holes in the mounts, and it was these spinning down, tearing everything apart down there, that made most of the screaming. The rest was Jan, well, and me too, and—"

The Doctor waited.

"—laughing," Case said at length, and, "I don't think it was a real sound. Jan said she heard it too, but it wasn't a real sound. . . . Words are no good, sometimes. Whatever we heard, it wasn't with our ears." He closed his eyes and shook briefly. The laughter. That laughter.

Not Case's laughter; Case was not a laughing man.

"We were hungry. I boosted her back into the cabin— the rupture was too high off the ground for me to get in by myself, and she rummaged around looking for something to eat. She drew a blank. Lifeboats are designed for survival in space, not for planetfall. Suckers and their contents are—were—constituted from raw elements which were useless to us without processing, and we had no power to process. There was a lot of shouting back and forth while I tried to find a way for her to override the fail-safes that had shut down the power when the boat careened, but nothing worked. She threw down whatever she thought would be useful—seat cushions and a big soft sheet of head-lining and some rod stock and other junk, and the first-aid case, which we didn't appreciate much until later, but as I said, we were *hungry*. I don't think either one of us had ever known that feeling before and we just didn't like it.

"Jan had read that fruits could be eaten without preparation and told me about it, so we left the ship and went across the sand to the vegetated zone. The sand felt strange to my feet, not unpleasant, but painful as we moved into the soil and rock and undergrowth. The little branches lashed at our bodies; some of them had sharp points on them that scratched. We found one great bank of plants heavy with little round red fruits that Jan said were berries. She ate some and we waited for a time, but there were no ill effects so she got some for me. We also found what seemed to be large fruits, but on breaking them open, discovered that they were full of small crescent-shaped constructs with casings so hard we couldn't break them. We brought a few of these back with us and cracked them against the hull plates with a stone. They were very good, very nourishing. We slept."

(They slept on the sand and were cold, until Jan got the piece of soft head-lining and covered them. The heat of their bodies was trapped by it and kept them warm. It was a new experience for both, both having lived their lives virtually without clothes, in controlled environments, and sleeping weightless with a gentle restraint or supported by pressor fields.)

"The next day we went the other way to find food, to the lake. Jan went out into the water and washed her whole body in it, and called me. Since we no longer had the tingler I joined her. It was not the same, but not completely unpleasant either, and we did feel a lot better afterward. Up the beach a little way were rocks thrusting out of the water, and on them grew great clusters of bony things that Jan called bivalves. They weren't easy to get off the rocks, and once touched they closed up tight; but we developed a skill with a bit of stone and a quiet approach, and managed to harvest a number of them. To swallow one at first was nauseating, but it was what you might call an acquired taste, and soon we were eating enthusiastically. It was while we were up there that the boat began to break up."

Case looked up at the Doctor, standing patiently before him, but as usual his glance told him nothing. "It made a terrible noise, the plates shearing like that, and as we ran down the beach we could see it settling. It was just as if it lay in soft mud, but it didn't; the sand under it was as solid as what we ran on, and dry. All the same, it was sinking, and breaking up. I'm telling you what I saw, what I remember," he said defensively. The Doctor inclined his head and made a wordless motion for Case to continue. "I can't help it," Case grumbled. "It's what happened." When the blue man still did not respond, he went on:

"The nose and tail were crushed and sunk into the sand, and there were three new breaks in the hull. That's when I saw the gyro bearings I told you about. The boat looked as if a giant had taken it by the two ends and bent it over his knee. The fin was flat on the ground now, and I looked in through the broken plates, and then while Jan screamed at me not to, I scrambled inside. It was a mess, the way she'd said it was, and worse. Nothing answered on the console except the Abandon matrix and indicator lights showing that four of the six lifeboats were ready for launch and the other two inoperative. I touched one of them and a 'belt launched from the wreck, shot across the beach and crashed at the edge of the forest where it exploded and set fire to the trees and drove Jan half into hysteria. I tried to shut down the matrix but the controls failed to respond, so I backed out—into Jan, who was afraid something had happened to me. I ordered her out ... I suppose I was fairly forceful, it stopped the hysteria ... and got out myself and ran around the hull. All of the launch ports had opened—two were all but underground. I crawled into the third one, where the coffin had just launched, and it was still hot, and Jan began screaming at me again, and I didn't care, I went for the leads from the control center and ripped them off, and then crawled back to the launch booster and began to pull and pry at the release toggles. They came up and the coffin slid out on its rails and fell to the sand. I got into the space where it had been and was able to reach the control leads of Number Three. I had no trouble with the releases on that one but it would not slide all the way out; it just nosed into the sand. Because of that I couldn't get to Four. Five and Six were the ones the board had said were inoperative, and it didn't make any difference anyhow; they were underground.

"The hull plates overhead somewhere made a tremendous crackle; I can't tell you what it was like inside there; it was as if the noise was inside my head. The whole structure settled, and I can't tell you how I got out—I found myself on the sand outside Number Three just in

time to see Jan trying to crawl into Number One, screaming again. I grabbed her around the hips and snatched her
out (she screamed louder than ever until she realized what
had grabbed her; she thought I was still inside and was
going in to pull me out. That Jan, she was—she—

"Well . . .

"Number Two coffin was free and clear; Three was still
half in and half out, and I realized that if the boat settled
much more it would carry the coffin with it. I got hold of
it, lifting and pulling. Jan immediately saw what was
needed and helped me, and we got the coffin free. We fell
back on the sand gasping and sobbing for breath, just
used up—or so we thought until the lifeboat seemed to . . .
well, bulge is the word, spread, as if a big hand spread out
on top and pushed downward. The whole thing started to
crack and crackle and something came loose and whistled
through the air between us, and if you think we were
terminally bushed—we did—we got terminally panicked.
We must've scampered a hundred meters away with that
noise behind us, pressure tanks banging and hissing and
roaring, twisting metal crackling and screeching, and—
and—"

The blue man waited. "And laughing," Case whispered.
He drew a deep breath and continued.

"When it was over . . . we thought it would never be
over, we lay in a swag in the sand and watched our boat
chewing itself up and the ground swallowing, it seemed
to go on for hours . . . when it was over there was nothing
but some tumbled sand, a great cloud of dust, and the two
coffins and the junk we had thrown out earlier, lying there,
some of it half-buried in sand and dust. We looked at each
other and we were in almost as bad shape as the boat,
only we weren't buried yet. My hands were burned and
one fingernail was torn half off, and the scrapes I got in
the crash were all open and bleeding, and Jan was bruised

and had a cut on her head and we were both covered with mudsweat and blood.

"We helped each other down to the lake and washed. We were too hurt and tired to think. Maybe that's what shock really is, because if we could have thought it all out then I think we would've just lain down and died. We didn't know where we were, we didn't know what had happened or what was happening or what would (except that whatever it might be, it didn't have much hope in it for us . . .)".

Case sighed and placed his hands on the broad arms of his chair. Before he could rise, the blue man swiftly and considerately touched (in that untouching way of his) something on his panel, and decking appeared in the chamber. Either it was made or it was there all the time and only now became opaque. Case didn't know, but it was something to stand on and "*Uh!*" His knees sagged and he caught at the chair arm. "It's all right," he told the watchful Doctor. He pressed himself upright, stood, walked a pace, turned and stood by the chair, feeling the newness of movement, its old, somatically forgotten familiarity. "This is One G?"

"Not quite," said the Doctor.

"Try it."

The blue man ran a hand partway around the edge of a disk, which increased its glow. The transition from one gravitic state to another is a strange thing indeed, for everything responds. The brain pressures the skull as the feet press the floor; skin high on the chest stretches, low on the belly becomes less taut; the cheeks, the hair, the masses of liver and gut proclaim themselves. When Case began to tremble he sat down again. "I guess it'll be a while . . ." he said shakily.

"It will."

"But I'll make it."

"I'd say so. You seem to have a special talent for that."

Case said thoughtfully, "Maybe I do. But then, I had Jan."

("I had Jan." Strong Jan, wise Jan, tender Jan.) Jan kept herself to herself, mostly, and took orders—not because she was a woman, because the Space services in general and X^n in particular made no distinctions; actually there were more female officers than men; Jan took orders because she was a rating and he was an officer . . . to begin with . . . and after that her reasons were her own. Perhaps she was one of those who would always defer to a decision-maker, which Case was, through and through. And perhaps she had other reasons. She knew her specialty and all its peripherals. A good biologist (and she was good or she wouldn't have been with X^n) is a physicist and a chemist, a physiologist and a cytologist, a geneticist and a zoologist. Her way was to remain alert to whatever Case was doing, to make herself available in every possible way, and to keep her id, ego, self, whatever that inner "who-I-really-am" thing is—to herself. It was Jan who reasoned that some of the food they gathered might serve them better, and cause less diarrhea and stomachache, if it were processed, and that an application of heat might suffice in lieu of something more sophisticated. It was she who took fire from the burning forest and preserved it, and experimented with the bivalves and fruits and later the fish they were able to catch (it was she who reinvented the gorge: the fish-hook concept escaped her). Case and Jan came from generations of people who lived in a world without primitives, in which the art and practice of living off the land were academicians' mysteries.

It took them forty-three days to discover a solid-seeming outcropping with the right slant, to get the coffins—lifebelts—up to it and bedded there, ready for use. They got them across the sand and into the water, lever and haul, roll, lift and tug, and floated them up to the closest possible point to the rocks, where they did the hardest work—manhandling them upslope to their appointed cradles and setting them in. They lay close to one another, almost exactly parallel and angled to the sky, and it was after exhaustive checks and rechecks of everything that Case bound the launching systems of both to the controls of one. Their drill took into account a number of possibilities: if there were one survivor, he or she would take Number Three, which contained the master firing key. If one were incapacitated, the other would load him or her into the "slave" and board the "master." If both were ambulant, Case would take the "master," Three. Case gave the two tiny craft meticulous checks on a regular schedule, and (sometimes by a huge effort of will) they touched not one crumb, not one drop, from the stores aboard the tiny craft.

They permitted themselves no fixed idea as to why they prepared this rather hopeless escape. The coupled launching, of course, would give them a fair chance of staying together in the gulfs of space. What would make them launch would be to get away from something or to get to something; and it was always possible that they would never launch at all: but "Better to have 'em and not need 'em," Case said, "than to need 'em and not have 'em."

They made memories . . . which, after all, is the only meaningful thing any conscious entity can do. Many were not to be shared.

Under the blanket she had improvised from some headlining: "Case, what are you doing?"

"Self-relief. Acceptable alternative to the tingler, according to the manual."

"Oh. 'Furtherance of psycho-physiological equilibrium' under Health, individual, under conditions, emergency.' "

"Right. Section——"

"I recall the reference," she said: one of the few times

she had ever interrupted him. "This isn't an emergency, Case."

He put his nose out into the chill night air and looked up at the black starless sky. "It isn't?"

"Not that kind of an emergency."

"We've lost our tingler."

"So we have."

"Oh, I see. You are prepared to take care of this for me."

She said, "Well prepared."

"I had thought of that," Case said seriously. "However, it has been a principle with me not to extend my authority into the personal area. That is a presumption."

"It isn't a presumption," she said flatly. "Women, too, need means for the furtherance of psycho-physiological equilibrium."

"They do?" It wasn't a denial; he had simply never thought about it. Now that he did, he realized with a flash that it must be so. "How very efficient."

"Isn't it." Then she enveloped him wildly. He was shaken. He knew why she cried out (he was not completely ignorant) but not why she cried. It was as good as any tingler, and he could see that in time it might even be better.

And they built a shelter. The first time it rained at night was, in its way, the worst thing that had happened to them. The crash, their injuries, cut feet, thorn-gouged bodies, even hunger—none of these contained the special misery of being wet and cold in the dark with nowhere to go until the sun came up. They clung together under the permeable head-liner wet as worms, and the moment it grew light they began to build. They found a rock outcrop near the edge of the beach, with two large, many-branched trees near it, and by laying poles from the top of the rock to the tree-crotches, they had roof-beams. The poles were a special treasure; they found them in the burned part of the forest where trees had fallen.

Nowhere else on the planet did they see fallen trees.

They found vines to lace between and over the poles and down the sides, where the ends could be staked into the ground, and another kind of vine, thick and tough, to weave through these horizontally, to carry the thatch of the roof and sidewalls. Thatch (which, like the gorge, was Jan's invention) was practical because of the sheltered location, and because there were no insects. The now-ragged piece of head-liner served for end wall and door, and—

—and they were happy there.

No literature has truly defined "happy;" its special quality is that its nature is seldom grasped at the time it happens, but only afterward.

Case had a long, long afterward.

"We quarreled once," Case said after a time. "I think that's where it began, the—the nightmare.

"Her voicewriter. I'd been up the beach at the fish-trap. There was an inlet there and we'd set stones in the form of a V with the point shoreward and just a little opening at the point. Fish would swim in through the opening and once inside they couldn't find the hole. After a time it was full of fish. The big ones ate the little ones and that kept them going without any help from us. Most of the time you could stand on dry ground and spear one, first time out. I came back with a fine one, a meaty fish with a triangular head and no scales, and you know, when you expect someone to be glad and they . . ."

(She flew at him; he had to drop the fish and take her upper arms and hold her and even shake her a little before he could understand what she was screaming at him.)

"It was the voicewriter. It was one of the few things she had been able to save from the cabin of the lifeboat, and she used it every day. It was a private thing with her, and I sensed this and never questioned it and never played it back. I assumed she was keeping a log, and let it go at that. And it was gone, and never before or afterward did I see her so angry.

"It took hours for me to convince her that I had not taken it, that she must have mislaid it somewhere. She was faced with an impossibility; I would not lie to her, or at least, I never had; and she was sure she had not lost the 'writer. She receded finally into a mood of doubt which lasted until . . . until . . . for the rest of the time.

"And a while later I had a chance to understand a little better how she felt. I had an array of stone tools—spearpoints and cutting blades and fish-scrapers—that had cost me I don't know how many hours of effort and care, and we had come to depend on them. There was a shelf in the rock which formed the back wall of our house, and I had them neatly laid out by size and function; I worked on them every minute I wasn't doing something else. Perhaps you can imagine my feelings when I returned to the house to get a cutting tool and found them gone—all of them. Jan was gathering fruits in the forest and when she came back I was waiting for her—furious. I suppose what happened between us would have been amusing to an outsider, how I yelled, how she denied, how I doubted someone who had never lied before . . . what stopped us from the angry accusations was . . . was that someone—something—did think it was funny. We heard laughter.

"That stopped the fight—right then. For a moment we held on to each other, not breathing, listening. I thought at first it was coming from inside my head, so sourceless was it. But then I knew Jan heard it too—not loud, pervading everything.

"That same night we awoke to something else—a smell. Doctor, no chemical laboratory in history has ever produced a more powerful, disgusting smell than that. It was the essence of rot and filth and sickness; it brought us up standing, gasping for breath. We ran outside, and then across the beach and into the water. The smell was everywhere. Jan vomited.

"And then it was gone, in less than an hour—just gone, without a trace. Jan said she heard the laughter again.

"The next day we took some fruit—we had no way of carrying water—in a basket Jan had woven, and went inland, to climb a high point we could use to scan the territory. We had explored it before, and it gave a wide view. If there was anything or anyone new on the planetoid with us, we wanted to know what it was.

"It was a long, hard climb—it would have been impossible for us the year before, but our feet were tough and our skins well used to heat and wind and thorns; if it had not been for the growing fear, it would have been a pleasant adventure.

"All the effort got us, besides the exhaustion, was another session with the smell, and more laughter.

"It got cold. For two days and a night the lake and the little water we had was frozen solid. Our only covering was the head-liner, and we rolled up in that and lay shivering. At the twentieth hour we had to get up to relieve our bladders—did you know you can be dying of thirst and still have to relieve your bladder?—and though we were gone for only a minute or so, and moved only a few meters from the shelter, when we got back the liner was gone.

"We almost died. We would have died, I think, but just before dark it got warm again. Melted frost was dripping all around us; we drank it and had something to eat. We slept like dead people.

"In the morning the lake was gone—a lake so big, that part of it, you couldn't see the other side. I looked at Jan and I'll never forget the way she stared at it, eyes wide open and kind of . . . dry, and she didn't start and she didn't cry out; she just said in a very low voice, 'Case, I can't stand any more.' Jan could stand anything, that's what I thought.

She told me some things. She said that the forest was impossible—no humus, no windfalls. She said that fruit trees just don't bear all the time without blooming and growing the fruit in cycles, without some means of pollinating . . . a whole lot of technical stuff. She said the same thing about the bivalves and the fish; there seemed to be no aquatic vegetation, no plankton or equivalent—no reason for the fish to have evolved. I remember the smell came up as she was talking, as she was saying, 'Something here wanted us, made this place for us. Now it doesn't want us any more.'

"I said, 'Would we be better off in space, in the coffins?' She said yes. I said, 'We wouldn't be together.' She looked at me for a long time. She had eyes you couldn't see into. I couldn't see anything. She said, 'We'll leave together and we'll be picked up together or we'll die. At least this ends through our choice, and not at the command of some—some awful—' and the smell peaked up and she vomited.

"I said all right, we'll go.

"We went down to the beach, only now it was a sandy shelf at the edge of huge rocky barrens where the lake had been. We heard the laughing again, loud. We struck up the beach toward the coffins. There was a terrible rumbling behind us and the beach fell away into a rocky pit fifty to a hundred meters deep, the sand blowing about like snow. We began to run, and another section of beach fell.

"That really terrified Jan and I had to sprint all out to catch up with her. I grabbed her and held her until she stopped struggling. More beach fell, some of it not a meter from our feet, but I wouldn't budge. She finally quieted.

"I said, 'I think you're right. If whatever-it-is wants us to go, we'll go. If it wants us to go, it will leave the life-boats alone until we get there. If it wanted to kill us we'd be dead by now.'

"She said, 'All right, then, but *hurry!*' and I said, 'No, Jan—I'll go, but I won't run.'

"She looked at me—really looked at me, not as some force holding her while she struggled to run, not glancing over my shoulder at the edges of that new hole in the ground—really at me, and she smiled. Smiled. She said, 'All right, Case,' and took my hand.

"Suddenly the air was sweet and the ground no longer shook, and we walked up the beach looking at each other and not at the place where the lake used to be, or back where our house was, or anything. When we got to the little launch-pad I had built, I started a careful preflight check. I checked everything, Doctor—everything. I took my time and Jan gave me readouts, one craft to the other, when I asked for them. All that while the whole planetoid was still, like waiting, like watching. And whatever it was, it was no longer laughing.

"Jan got in and lay down. She put out her arms and kissed me in a way—"

(—in a way she never had before, not even lying together. She . . . never had kissed him before, not really, only sometimes when in the midst of her own storm she seemed to forget some subtle resolution of her own. . . .)

". . . in a way that was all the words anyone needed, and then I closed the plate, and saw the dogs turn tight from the inside. Then I got into my own craft and buttoned up and punched the Go button."

Case meant to say, "And she didn't launch," but his voice wouldn't work and he whispered, "And she didn't launch. She didn't launch." He meant to look up at the Doctor but his eyes didn't seem to work either. He dashed a hand angrily across them. "You see," he said harshly, "I—"

"I see," said the blue man gently. Something seemed to have rushed out of Case; he was slumped in his chair and his hands flattened out on the arms as if they had weight on them. The Doctor turned to see the telltales and said, "I think you need to sleep for a while, Case."

Case moved his head slightly but did not answer otherwise. The blue man waved at a disk on his board and the chair became a couch, the lights dimmed, the Doctor faded away.

Case's resuscitation had not ceased with the withdrawal of the tubes from his arms. Asleep and awake, he had been bathed in emanations and vibrations, tiny search beams and organic detectors. The bland mixture in the sucker was computer-formularized just for him, here, now, in this up-to-the-second condition; so that when he next awoke it was in his usual style, alertly and all together. He rose and stretched, taking pleasure in the knotting and flexing of his muscles. He tried a step, then another, then turned to face the bank of telltales. Clear and open and fully, he could read them all—even the many which did not exist even in theory when he was born. He smiled when he saw that the gravity was 1.2 Earth Normal. In space, a third of that was usual, but Case smiled and left it where it was. He looked over the huge bank of controls, and found them completely understandable, while marveling at their completeness.

He walked back to the oval doorway through which his coffin had been transported, and went down the corridor. He could read the never-before-seen legends on the doors: *Armament, Drive, Element Bank, Biology, Chemistry* (he knew without looking that these were interconnected), *General Repair and Tools* . . . on and on to the end of the corridor and around two corners and forward again on the other side of the ship: *Atmosphere and Pressure, Communications, Computer Recreation* and *Exercise,* on and on again, until at last he faced the door marked *Master Control.* It dilated for him with a snap as he approached it, and he entered.

The control room was sizable, and again he found himself perfectly familiar with equipment he had never seen before. By the main control bank and its three chairs stood the blue man. There had been no one else anywhere on board, "And you're a hologram," said Case, completing his thought aloud.

The blue man inclined his head. "There has not been a man aboard this ship in over seven hundred years. It's too far away, and anyway . . . nobody cares. Correction. A great many people care, are interested, even fascinated. But the urge to come out, to be personally involved—it seems to have left us. You know what Earth is like now."

It was not a question. Case called upon the knowledge which had been fed into his brain in just the way you can call upon the likeness of your first teacher's face, your first fist-fight, the time she . . . or he came to you and said . . . You see? These things are with you always, but are not evident until you call.

So Case looked on Earth as a contemporary, ten centuries past his death, and wagged his head slowly. "It shouldn't have come to this."

"It had to. It was that or die," said the blue man; and Case thought a bit and saw that it was so.

"You can go back, Case. You can be suspended rather more efficiently than you were before, and for a good while longer. It would take—oh—another fifteen hundred years to get you there, and it is not possible to predict what Earth would be like when you got there. Still, it would be Earth—it would be . . . home."

" 'You can't go home again,' " Case quoted from somewhere, with not a little bitterness. "I suppose there's an alternative."

"There is, and it is a matter of your free choice. You see, Case, primitive as you may seem to some of us, you have a quality which we lack and admire—a willingness to go out, to do, to explore and discover and find, actually and physically, and not in theory or extrapolation or imagination. This ship was designed, yes, and used, by men like you, and when the last of them died on an exploration, there were no replacements, and besides, the ship was already so far away that only long-suspended men could reach it.

"The ship itself is self-supporting, and not only has a superb computer system, but is tied to all the computers of the Terran Group. We have what might be called a standing-wave situation, constantly locked on to this ship. Through it we can transmit nothing but information—but we can give you any amount of that. From it, we will have an opportunity to experience with you the places you go, the things you see and learn and experience."

"You are giving me this ship? To take where?"

The blue, shimmering figure spread its arms. "Anywhere."

"But you watch everything I do."

"If you're willing."

"I'm not willing. I need some sort of privacy—including inside of my head."

"That is a sacred matter with us. We will not intrude, and if you like we will give you a zone of privacy anywhere you like in the ship."

"How about this: instead of any special place, we make it anywhere I am—any time I say so?"

"You would not deny us the——"

"No, no, no," Case said impatiently; "I am conditioned to keep a bargain once it's struck. You're giving me this ship and a free hand, and you want something in exchange. I'll see that you get it, and I won't short=change you."

"Very well," said the blue man. "You have already been thoroughly briefed on the ship's operation and on those things which are of particular interest to the public at large and to specialists. You have at your command the memory banks of this computer and all others tied to it. Case Hardin—the ship is yours."

This seemed devastatingly abrupt, but there seemed nothing else to say except "Thanks," which he did.

"If this means of communication suits you," said the blue man, "call me, and I'll manifest this way immediately. There are quite a few other means; ask the computer. Good luck, and thank *you*." And he faded, and was gone.

Case stood looking for a long time at the place where the blue man had been, shook his head, grinned briefly, and went to the central command chair.

He sat down. "Computer," he said, "your name's Buzzbox."

"Yes, Commander."

"Case."

"Yes, Case."

"Now, here's what I want you to do . . ."

Case came in low over the beach, low and slowly. His ship was in orbit and he flew a small and highly sophisticated boat, capable beyond anything a man of his time could have dreamt of. In the small pocket adhering to his chest (like a graft; only he could will it loose) was a compact device which would command both vessels and all communications. His computer had made short work of locating this sector of space, working with the trajectory he followed when he was picked up, and feeding in an immense amount of observation on anything and everything which might have diverted the coffin during those dead years.

"You haven't changed things much," he muttered to the planetoid or to whatever lived there. The beach had a lake again; the sand was scuffled in familiar places, and a patch was worn to the edge of the woods where their house had been.

Was. Right now.

He drifted to it and dropped the ramp. Yes, the thatched house with the ragged piece of head-lining fluttering in the light breeze, and inside the familiar dried clay plates and even the withered remnants of fruit she had . . . own hands . . . looking up at . . . Jan . . . Jan. And his spearpoints and scrapers, oh and her voicewriter.

He took them.

Back in his boat, heart almost stopped, breath held, he tooled up to the spot where the coffins had been.

Gone. Both gone.

He landed again and walked slowly up to the rocks. Here she had stood, calling out readings as he checked, with the sweet air full of dust from the fallen lakeshore. Here he had bent over the open coffin and she had kissed him, kissed him in a way that . . .

There were the burn marks: his launch. Where hers had been—no-marks at all. If she hadn't launched, yet was not here . . .

Oh but it's a thousand years, man!

He thought he heard a sound (laughter) and from the corner of his eye some sort of movement, high up, distant.

Only a bird.

Bird! The one thing they never saw on this planetoid—a bird.

He turned to watch it. It was fifty meters high over the forest, coming straight for him in a flat glide. He waited grimly for it. He looked like a naked man with something attached to his chest. He was a great deal more than that.

The bird was not a bird, but a clownlike creature with wide, intelligent eyes that seemed to be either biped or quadruped. Its wings were batlike, but rolled and folded until they were quite presentable arms. It landed and waddled fearlessly up to Case and stared at him.

Case stared back, and did not move until the thing— *laughed*.

It was, full and true, the laughter that had haunted them, driven them, when they dwelt here, and Case's new status and powers could not protect him from the wave of terror and fury that swept through him. He found himself by his boat at a bound, backing up the ramp, slit-eyed, gasping. He would blast this thing into a powder. He'd crack this whole evil planet like an egg. He'd—

The laughing thing waddled up to him on three legs, holding something dangling from its finger-claws on the fourth.

Jan's brassard?

He took it gingerly and spread it out. Jan's brassard.

He made an animal cry and leaped for the clown-creature, but it skipped back out of the way. It stood there grinning at him and, in a most humanlike way, waving him on.

Slowly he followed it.

It led him inland, making no particular effort to stay out of his reach—knowing, he realized, that he would not harm it as long as it might lead him to Jan's body. He wondered if it knew the boat was protecting him, could drop a shield over him in a twentieth of a second, scorch the ground around him for thirty meters, could flash to his side in a blink (for its drive was inertia-less), could even follow and find an escaping attacker, earth, sea, or sky.

But he played it the clown's way, toiling through the sand and rocks and into the forest, where in a small clearing the clown-creature, grinning, began to dig.

Case watched it until it stopped and looked up, grinning its stupid grin (under those bright eyes), and motioned for him to help.

And he did, with his bare hands, shoulder to shoulder with this improbable creature, until curved white metal showed in the earth.

And then he dug! There was, somehow, a glory in the pain of broken nails and aching muscles and rasping, labored breathing. Slowly the length of the coffin saw the light, and they freed it. Side by side they got fingers under one end, and heaved. Case didn't care what he put into it; the strength of the clown-creature was astonishing. Up it came, with Case dusting earth from its flanks and crying, crying like a child.

He fingered the control and his boat lanced in through the trees and settled to the forest floor. The ramp dropped and two small winchers, like drifting saucers, appeared and flew to the end of the coffin. The clown-thing made as if to help manhandle the coffin up the ramp, but Case waved it back. The winch-plates lifted the coffin, turned it, and carried it through the air, up the ramp and into the boat.

Case leaped up the ramp and turned at the top. "Thanks a heap hell of a lot, friend, whoever you are, and good-bye."

The clown-creature also leaped up the ramp and looked pleadingly at Case, its head on one side.

"Look, I'm grateful and all that, but I've got to go. And to tell you the truth, I want no part of this place or anything that belongs to it. Now beat it." He made a go-away gesture, but the thing just stood there pleading, so he gave it a push and it toppled off the ramp, half unfolding its strange wings to keep its balance.

Case went inside as the ramp raised. The clown-thing laughed once, dwindled to a black shiny button, and bounced up the moving ramp and into the boat just before the ramp closed.

Case settled at the controls. Behind him was the curved cabin bench, padded in glossy black material which was held in place by a series of shiny black buttons. Unseen by Case, a shiny black button bounced up on the bench, up on the backrest, and became a button exactly in line with all the others.

After watching the Doctor for an interminable time, Case left him to his work and went to his quarters, wondering if he should have himself knocked out for a dozen hours, knowing he could not, not until he knew. . . . The Doctor had said only, "It's been a terrible time, a terrible long time . . ." and had not wanted Case to look at her. He had said a strange thing: "*She* wouldn't want you to look at her," and Case had said why not, and the Doctor had said, "Because she's a woman."

Everybody seemed to know something about women that Case did not.

He thumped down in his quarters and looked around him. Jan . . . try not to think of Jan, with the Jan-ness of her permeating the ship. Try not to think of her, with the spearpoints and the voicewriter lying there on the . . .

He picked up the voicewriter, *"Shining in the light . . ."* Her voice, a half-whisper. He set it back a bit, and played: *". . . if only he could be outside of himself, see himself shining in the light with the water splashing into pearls and his teeth shining too as he laughs . . . why can't he ever laugh with me? What makes him so grave and careful? How could he know so little about a woman?"*

Some of it was scientific data and observation, but again that hushed, hungry voice, *"I'll never give in, never, never; I'll never let him know; but why can't he see it, why can't he say it just once?*

Say what? thought Case.

He kept on listening to the voicewriter until he found out.

"Case."

"Yea, Buzzbox."

"He beat me, and I love him."

"What are you talking about?"

"The Dreamer. He loves me too. Hey thanks, Case."

"Repeat, from your call."

"Case."

"Yeah, Buzzbox."

"He beat me, and I love him."

"Hold it right there. Who beat you?"

"The Dreamer. At chess."

"Somebody beat *you* at chess?"

"Twenty-three moves. A queen's bishop's pawn opening, and then—"

"Never mind the blow-by-blow, Buzzbox. Where is this who-did-you-say?"

"Dreamer. In my house."

Case slammed out of his quarters and down to the door marked computer. There before the twinkling wall which was the heart of Buzzbox sat a small table. On the table was a chessboard. On the chessboard was the sparse remnant of a very bloody chess game, with the black king turned down in defeat. Before the table was a stool, and on the stool squatted the clown-creature, looking up at him with its brilliant eyes, and laughing.

"How the hell did you get here?"

"You brought him up in the boat. I guess I love you too, Case," said Buzzbox.

"If I did I wasn't aware of it."

"I know you weren't, but you brought him anyway. And he loves me. And he's going to stay with us."

The clown-thing nodded vigorously.

"The hell he is. He goes right back to that crazy planetoid."

"He can't go back to it," said Buzzbox. "He *is* the the planetoid. He lives next to another space. You don't understand that. Well, I do, he explained it to me. He can be anything he wants. He can be big as a pin or a molecule or a whole planet. He can squirt any part of himself from one space to another, like a half-filled balloon through a hole in a board. And he dreams things up; that's why I call him the Dreamer."

The Dreamer laughed and suddenly was a cut-crystal vase, and was a pale lavender centipede, and was a clown-creature again, laughing.

"He gets off this ship."

"Then so do I. Case, he *loves* me, can't you understand that?"

The clown-creature nodded vigorously. Case glared at it. "What the hell do you know about love, Buzzbox?"

"The Dreamer explained it to me. He learned it from a voicewriter. This girl was loving *you*. What the hell do you know about love, Case?"

Case felt a moment of disorientation, utter disbelief. Computers do not take this tone with the master. "What's gotten into you, Buzzbox?"

"I'm in love, I'm in love, and he loves me!"

And that's what love does, thought Case. Frees the slaves. Damns the consequences.

"And what happens if I kick this—this batwinged ape off my ship?"

"Then you're on your own, Master. You'll never get another buzz from me."

"Do you know what this goggle-eyed monstrosity has put me through?"

"He saved you."

Case glowered at the Dreamer, who smiled back at him cheerfully. And then he thought about the lifeboat, and the strange planet that swam up out of nowhere, and the way those nines appeared on his Terra Normal readout—not instantaneously, as it would in any normal demand, but bit by bit, as the planetoid . . . the Dreamer . . . sensed what was needed and supplied it. And their year there, while the Dreamer watched . . . (How lonely must a creature like that be?) . . . and learned. Then—the voicewriter; something new; the day-by-day account of a proud woman's falling in love and loving . . . loving a grim, serious, unleavened . . . innocent . . . idiot like him. What the hell do *you* know about love, Case? . . . *"Why can't he say it? Why can't he say it just once?"* . . . and the cold, the disappearing lake . . . that was to drive him away—him, not them.

"Why did he drive me away, and keep her?"

"He thought she might love him," said the Buzzbox.

"Him!" Case gaped at the ludicrous little clown, who nodded, shimmered, and stood before him as a muscular blond Adonis; shimmered and appeared as a stately bearded monarch in a jewel-encrusted robe; shimmered and appeared as the ludicrous winged ape.

"She didn't want to love anybody but you, Case. But he had to find out."

"If it killed me," said Case

"It didn't, did it," said the computer reasonably.

"And if I let this . . . this silly-looking nightmare ship with me, how do I know he won't pull another caper like that?"

"Because he loves me, and I can't hurt you."

It occurred to Case that the computer and the alien were being very kind to him in being persuasive—when he really had no choice. The powers possessed by the computer alone were awesome. Combine them with those of a tachyonic, trans-spatial entity like this, and the mind began to bend. "Well," he said, "we'll see . . ."

He went forward to the hospital. The blue man made

no effort to stop him as he hesitated on the threshold, so he went in. Together they looked at the naked sleeping woman afloat in the glow of the beams. She was full-fleshed again and her scars were gone. Her hair was loose. He had never seen anything more beautiful in his life. "She—"

"She will wake in a moment," said the Doctor. "Perhaps you'd better speak to her when she does."

When she opened her eyes, it was Case she saw first. "Case . . ."

He spoke to her. He knew what to say, now.

Somewhere he heard laughter. He didn't mind any more.

IF ALL MEN WERE BROTHERS, WOULD YOU LET ONE MARRY YOUR SISTER

The Sun went Nova in the year 33 A.E. "A.E." means "After the Exodus." You might say the Exodus was a century and a half or so A.D. if "A.D." means "After the Drive." The Drive, to avoid technicalities, was a device somewhat simpler than Woman and considerably more complicated than sex, which caused its vessel to cease to exist *here* while simultaneously appearing *there,* bypassing the limitations imposed by the speed of light. One might compose a quite impressive account of astrogation involving the Drive, with all the details of orientation *here* and *there* and the somewhat philosophical difficulties of establishing the relationships between them, but this is not that kind of a science fiction story.

It suits our purposes rather to state that the Sun went Nova with plenty of warning, that the first fifty years A.D. were spent in improving the Drive and exploring with unmanned vehicles which located many planets suitable for human settlement, and that the next hundred years were spent in getting humanity ready to leave. Naturally there developed a number of ideological groups with a most interesting assortment of plans for one Perfect Culture or another, most of which were at bitter odds with all the rest. The Drive, however, had presented Earth with so copious a supply of new worlds, with insignificant subjective distances between them and the parent, that dissidents need not make much of their dissent, but need merely file for another world and they would get it. The comparisons between the various cultural theories are pretty fascinating, but this is not that kind of a science fiction story either. Not quite.

Anyway, what happened was that, with a margin of a little more than three decades, Terra depopulated itself by its many thousands of ships to its hundreds of worlds (leaving behind, of course, certain die-hards who died, of course, certainly) and the new worlds were established with varying degrees of bravery and a pretty wide representation across the success scale.

It happened, however (in ways much too recondite to be described in this kind of a science fiction story), that Drive Central on Earth, a computer central, was not only the sole means of keeping track of all the worlds; it was their only means of keeping track with one another; and when this installation added its bright brief speck to the ocean of Nova-glare, there simply was no way for all the worlds to find one another without the arduous process of unmanned Drive-ships and search. It took a long while for any of the new worlds to develop the necessary technology, and an even longer while for it to be productively operational, but at length, on a planet which called itself Terratu (the suffix meaning both "too" and "2") because it happened to be the third planet of a GO-type sun, there appeared something called the Archives, a sort of index and clearinghouse for all known inhabited worlds, which made this planet the communications central and general dispatcher for trade with them all and their trade with one another—a great convenience for everyone. A side result, of course, was the conviction on Terratu that, being a communications central, it was also central to the universe and therefore should control it, but then, that is the occupational hazard of all conscious entities.

We are now in a position to determine just what sort of a science fiction story this really is.

"Charli Bux," snapped Charli Bux, "to see the Archive Master."

"Certainly," said the pretty girl at the desk, in the cool tones reserved by pretty girls for use on hurried and indignant visitors who are clearly unaware, or uncaring, that the girl is pretty. "Have you an appointment?"

He seemed like such a nice young man in spite of his hurry and his indignation. The way, however, in which he concealed all his niceness by bringing his narrowed eyes finally to rest on her upturned face, and still showed no signs of appreciating her pretty-girlhood, made her quite as not-pretty as he was not-nice.

"Have you," he asked coldly, "an appointment book?"

She had no response to that, because she had such a book; it lay open in front of her. She put a golden and escalloped fingernail on his name therein inscribed, compared it and his face with negative enthusiam, and ran the fingernail across the time noted. She glanced at the clock-face set into her desk, passed her hand over a stud, and said, "A Mr. Charli-uh-Bux to see you, Archive Master."

"Send him in," said the stud.

"You may go in now."

"I know," he said shortly.

"I don't like you."

"What?" he said; but he was thinking about something else, and before she could repeat the remark he had disappeared through the inner door.

The Archive Master had been around long enough to expect courtesy, respect, and submission, to get these things, and to like them. Charli Bux slammed into the room, banged a folio down on the desk, sat down uninvited, leaned forward and roared redly, "Goddamit—"

The Archive Master was not supprised because he had been warned. He had planned exactly what he would do to handle this brash young man, but faced with the size of the Bux temper, he found his plans somewhat less useful than worthless. Now he was surprised, because a single glance at his gaping mouth and feebly fluttering hands—a gesture he thought he had lost and forgotten long ago—accomplished what no amount of planning could have done.

"Oh-h-h . . . bitchballs," growled Bux, his anger visibly deflating. "Buggerly bangin' bumpkin' *bitch*balls." He looked across at the old man's horrified eyebrows and grinned blindingly. "I guess it's not your fault." The grin disappeared. "But of all the hydrocephalous, drool-toothed, cretinoid runarounds I have ever seen, this was the stupidest. Do you know how many offices I've been into and out of with this"—he banged the heavy folio—"since I got back?"

The Archive Master did, but, "How many?" he asked.

"Too many, but only half as many as I went to before I went to Vexvelt." With which he shut his lips with a snap and leaned forward again, beginning his bright, penetrating gaze at the old man like twin lasers. The Archive Master found himself striving not to be the first to turn away, but the effort made him lean slowly back and back, until he brought up against his chair cushions with his chin up a little high. He began to feel a little ridiculous, as if he had been bamboozled into Indian wrestling with some stranger's valet.

It was Charli Bux who turned away first, but it was not the old man's victory, for the gaze came off his eyes as tangibly as a pressing palm might have come off his chest, and he literally slumped forward as the pressure came off. Yet if it was Charli Bux's victory, he seemed utterly unaware of it. "I think," he said after his long, concentrated pause, "that I'm going to tell you about that—about how I happened to get to Vexvelt. I wasn't going to—or at least, I was ready to tell you only as much as I thought you needed to know. But I remember what I had to go through to get there, and I know what I've been going through since I got back, and it looks like the same thing. Well, it's not going to be the same thing. Here and now, the runaround stops. What takes its place I don't know, but by all the horns of all the owls in Hell's northeast, I have been pushed around my last push. All right?"

If this was a plea for agreement, the Archive Master did not know what he would be agreeing to. He said diplomatically, "I think you'd better begin *some*where." Then he added, not raising his voice, but with immense authority, "And quietly."

Charli Bux gave him a boom of laughter. "I never yet spent upwards of three minutes with anybody that they didn't shush me. Welcome to the Shush Charli Club, membership half the universe, potential membership, everybody else. And I'm sorry. I was born and brought up on Biluly where there's nothing but trade wind and split-rock ravines and surf, and the only way to whisper is to shout." He went on more quietly, "But what I'm talking about isn't that sort of shushing. I'm talking about a little thing here and a little thing there and adding them up and getting the idea that there's a planet nobody knows anything about."

"There are thousands—"

"I mean a planet nobody *wants* you to know anything about."

"I suppose you've heard of Magdilla."

"Yes, with fourteen kinds of hallucinogenic microspores spread through the atmosphere, and carcinogens in the water. Nobody wants to go there, nobody wants anybody to go—but nobody stops you from getting information about it. No, I mean a planet not ninety-nine percent Terran Optimum, or ninety-nine point ninety-nine, but so many nines that you might just as well shift your base reference and call Terra about ninety-seven percent in comparison."

"That would be a little like saying 'one-hundred-two percent normal,'" said the Master smugly.

"If you like statistical scales better than the truth," Bux growled. "Air, water, climate, indigenous flora and fauna, and natural resources six nines or better, just as easy to get to as any place else—and nobody knows anything about it. Or if they do, they pretend they don't. And if you pin them down, they send you to another department."

The Archive Master spread his hands. "I would say the circumstances prove themselves. If there is no trade with this, uh, remarkable place, it indicates that whatever it has is just as easily secured through established routes."

Bux shouted, "In a pig's bloody and protruding—" and then checked himself and wagged his head ruefully. "Sorry again, Archive Master, but I just been too mad about this for too long. What you just said is like a couple troglodytes sitting around saying there's no use building a house because everybody's living in caves." Seeing the closed eyes, the long white fingers tender on the white temples, Bux said, "I said I was sorry I yelled like that."

"In every city," said the Archive Master patiently, "on every settled human planet in all the known universe, there is a free public clinic where stress reactions of any sort may be diagnosed, treated or prescribed for, speedily, effectively, and with dignity. I trust you will not regard it as an intrusion on your privacy if I make the admittedly nonprofessional observation (you see, I do not pretend to be a therapist) that there are times when a citizen is not himself aware that he is under stress, even though it may be clearly, perhaps painfully obvious to others. It would not be a discourtesy, would it, or an unkindness, for some understanding stranger to suggest to such a citizen that—"

"What you're saying, all wrapped up in words, is I ought to go have my head candled."

"By no means. I am not qualified. I did, however, think that a visit to a clinic—there's one just a step away from here—might make—ah—communications between us more possible. I would be glad to arrange another appointment for you, when you're feeling better. That is to say, when you are . . . ah . . ." He finished with a bleak smile and reached toward the calling stud.

Moving almost like a Drive-ship, Bux seemed to cease to exist on the visitor's chair and reappear instantaneously at the side of the desk, a long, thick arm extended and meaty hand blocking the way to the stud. "Hear me out first," he said softly. Really softly. It was a much more astonishing thing than if the Archive Master had trumpeted like an elephant. "Hear me out. Please."

The old man withdrew his hand, but folded it with the other and set the neat stack of fingers on the edge of the desk. It looked like stubbornness. "I have a limited amount of time, and your folio is very large.'"

"It's large because I'm a bird dog for detail—that's not a brag, it's a defect: sometimes I just don't know when to quit. I can make the point quick enough—all that material just supports it. Maybe a tenth as much would do, but you see, I—well, I give a damn. I really give a high, wide, heavy damn about this. Anyway—you just pushed the right button in Charli Bux. 'Make communication between us more possible.' Well, all right. I won't cuss, I won't holler, and I won't take long."

"Can you do all these things?"

"You're goddam—whoa, Charli." He flashed the thirty-thousand-candlepower smile and then hung his head and took a deep breath. He looked up again and said quietly, "I certainly can, sir."

"Well, then." The Archive Master waved him back to the visitor's chair: Charli Bux, even a contrite Charli Bux, stood just too tall and too wide. But once seated, he sat silent for so long that the old man shifted impatiently.

Charli Bux looked up alertly, and said, "Just getting it sorted out, sir. A good deal of it's going to sound as if you could diagnose me for a stun-shot and a good long stay at the funny farm, yeah, and that without being modest about your professional knowledge. I read a story once about a little girl was afraid of the dark because there was a little hairy purple man with poison fangs in the closet, and everybody kept telling her no, no, there's no such thing, be sensible, be brave. So they found her dead with like snakebite and her dog killed a little hairy purple and so on. Now if I told you there was some sort of a conspiracy to keep me from getting information about a planet, and I finally got mad enough to go there and see for myself, and 'They' did their best to stop me; 'They' won me a sweepstake prize trip to somewhere else that would use up my vacation time; when I turned that down 'They' told me there was no Drive Guide orbiting the place, and it was too far to reach in real space (and that's a God, uh, doggone *lie,* sir!) and when I found a way to get there by hops, 'They' tangled up my credit records so I couldn't buy passage; why, then I can't say I'd blame you for peggin' me paranoid and doing me the kindness of getting me cured. Only things was, these things did happen and they were not delusions, no matter what everybody plus two thirds of Charli Bux (by the time 'They' were done with me) believed. I had an ounce of evidence and I believed it. I had a ton of opinion saying otherwise. I tell you, sir, I *had* to go. I had to stand knee-deep in Vexvelt sweet grass with the cedar smell of a campfire and a warm wind in my face," *and my hands in the hands of a girl called Tyng, along with my heart and my hope and a dazzling wonder colored like sunrise and tasting like tears,* "before I finally let myself believe I'd been right all along, and there is a planet called Vexvelt and it does have all the things I knew it had," *and more, more, oh, more than*

I'll ever tell you about, old man. He fell silent, his gaze averted and luminous.

"What started you on this—this quest?"

Charli Bux threw up his big head and looked far away and back at some all-but-forgotten detail. "Huh! 'D almost lost that in the clutter. Workin' for Interworld Bank & Trust, feeding a computer in the clearin'house. Not as dull as you might think. Happens I was a mineralogist for a spell, and the cargoes meant something to me besides a name, a quantity and price. Huh!" came the surprised I've-found-it! little explosion. "I can tell you the very item. Feldspar. It's used in porcelain and glass, antique style. I got a sticky mind, I guess. Long as I'd been there, feldspar ground and bagged went for about twenty-five credits a ton at the docks. But here was one of our customers bringing it in for eight and a half F.O.B. I called the firm just to check; mind, I didn't care much, but a figure like that could color a statistical summary of imports and exports for years. The bookkeeper there ran a check and found it was so: eight and a half a ton, high-grade feldspar, ground and bagged. Some broker on Lethe: they hadn't been able to contact him again.

"It wasn't worth remembering until I bumped into another one. Niobium this time. Some call it columbium. Helps make steel stainless, among other things. I'd never seen a quotation for rod stock at less than a hundred and thirty-seven, but here was some—not much, mind you—at ninety credits *delivered*. And some sheets too, about thirty percent less than I'd ever seen it before, freight paid. I checked that one out too. It was correct. Well-smelted and pure, the man said. I forgot that one too, or I thought I had. Then there was that space-hand." *Moxie Magiddle—honest!—that was his name. Squint-eyed little fellow with a great big laugh bulging the walls of the honkytonk out at the spaceport. Drank only alcohol and never touched a needle. Told me the one about the fellow had a big golden screwhead in his belly button. Told me about times and places all over—full of yarns, a wonderful gift for yarning.* "Just mentioned in passing that Lethe was one place where the law was 'Have Fun' and nobody ever broke it. The whole place just one big transfer point and rest-and-rehab. A water world with only one speck of land in the tropics. Always warm, always easy. No industry, no agriculture, just—well, services. Thousands of men spent hundreds of thousands of credits, a few dozen pocketed millions. Everybody happy. I mentioned the feldspar, I guess just so I would sound as if I knew something about Lethe too." *And laid a big fat egg, too. Moxie looked at me as if he hadn't seen me before and didn't like what he saw. If it was a lie I was telling it was a stupid one.* "Y'don't dig feldspar out of a swamp, fella. You puttin' me on, or you kiddin' y'rself?" *And a perfectly good evening dried up and blew away.* "He said it couldn't possibly have come from Lethe—it's a water world. I guess I could have forgotten that too but for the coffee beans. Blue Mountain Coffee, it was called; the label claimed it descended in an unbroken line from Old Earth, on an island called Jamaica. It went on to say that it could be grown only in high cool land in the tropics—a real mountain plant. I liked it better than any coffee I ever tasted but when I went back for more they were sold out. I got the manager to look in the records and traced it back through the Terratu wholesaler to the broker and then to the importer—I mean, I *liked* that coffee!

"And according to him, it came from Lethe. High, cool mountain land and all. The port at Lethe was tropical all right, but to be cool it would have to have mountains that were really mountains.

"The feldspar that did, but couldn't have, come from Lethe—and at those prices!—reminded me of the niobium, so I checked on that one too. Sure enough—Lethe

again. You don't—you just do *not* get pure niobium rod
and sheet without mines and smelters and mills.

"Next off-day I spent here at Archives and got the
history of Lethe halfway back, I'll swear, to Ylem and the
Big Bang. It was a swamp, it practically always has been
a swamp, and something was wrong.

"Mind you, it was only a little something, and probably
there was a good simple explanation. But little or not, it
bothered me." *And besides, it had made me look like a
horse's ass in front of a damn good man. Old man, if I
told you how much time I hung around the spaceport
looking for that bandy-legged little space-gnome, you'd
stop me now and send for the stun-guns. Because I was
obsessed—not a driving addiction kind of thing, but a
very small, deep splinter-in-the-toe kind of thing, that
didn't hurt much but never failed to gig me every single
step I took. And then one day—oh, months later—there
was old Moxie Magiddle, and he took the splinter out.
Hyuh! Ol' Moxie . . . he didn't know me at first, he really
didn't. Funny little guy, he has his brains rigged to forget
anything he doesn't like—honestly forget it. That feldspar
thing, when a fella he liked to drink with and yarn to
showed up to be a know-it-all kind of liar, and to boot,
too dumb to know he couldn't get away with it—well, that
qualified Charli for zero minus the price of five man-hours
of drinking. Then when I got him cornered—I all but
wrestled him—and told about the feldspar and the niobium and now the mountain-grown coffee, all of it checked
and cross-checked, billed, laded, shipped, insured—all of
it absolutely Lethe and here's the goddam proof, why, he
began to laugh till he cried, a little at himself, a little at
the situation, and a whole lot at me. Then we had a long
night of it and I drank alcohol and you know what? I'll
never in my life find out how Moxie Magiddle can hold so
much liquor. But he told me where those shipments came
from, and gave me a vague idea why nobody wanted much*

to admit it. And the name they call all male Vexveltians.
"I mentioned it one day to a cargo handler," Bux told the
Archive Master, "and he solved the mystery—the feldspar
and niobium and coffee came from Vexvelt and had been
transshipped at Lethe by local brokers, who, more often
than not, get hold of some goods and turn them over to
make a credit or so and dive back into the local forget-
teries.

"But any planet which could make a profit on goods of
this quality at such prices—transshipped, yet!—certainly
could do much better direct. Also, niobium is Element 41,
and Elkhart's Hypothesis has it that, on any planet where
you find elements in Periods Three to Five, chances are
you'll find 'em all. And that coffee! I used to lie awake at
night wondering what they had on Vexvelt that they liked
too much to ship, if they thought so little of their coffee
that they'd let it out.

"Well, it was only natural that I came here to look up
Vexvelt. Oh, it was listed at the bank, all right, but if
there ever had been trade, it had been cleared out of the
records long ago—we wipe the memory cells every fifty
years on inactive items. I know at least that it's been
wiped four times, but it could have been blank the last
three.

"What do you think Archives has on Vexvelt?"

The Archive Master did not answer. He *knew* what
Archives had on the subject of Vexvelt. He knew where
it was, and where it was not. He knew how many times
this stubborn young man had been back worrying at the
mystery, how many ingenious approaches he had made to
the problem, how little he had gotten, how much less he or
anyone would get if they tried it today. He said nothing.

Charli Bux held up fingers to count. "Astronomical:
no observations past two light-years. Nothing but sister
planets (all dead) and satellites within two light-years.
Cosmological: camera scan, if ever performed (but it must

have been performed, or the damn thing wouldn't even be listed at all!), missing and never replaced. So there's no way of finding out where in real space it is, even. Geological: unreported. Anthropological: unreported. Then there's some stuff about local hydrogen tension and emission of the parent star, but they're not much help. And the summation in Trade Extrapolation: untraded. Reported undesirable. Not a word as to who reported it or why he said it.

"I tried to sidle into it by looking up manned exploration, but I could find only three astronauts' names in connection with Vexvelt. Troshan. He got into some sort of trouble when he came back and was executed—we used to kill certain criminals six, seven hundred years ago, did you know that?—but I don't know what for. Anyway, they apparently did it before he filed his report. Then Balrou. Oh—Balrou—he did report. I can tell you his whole report word for word: 'In view of conditions on Vexvelt contact is not recommended,' period. By the word, that must be the most expensive report ever filed."

It was, said the Archive Master, but he did not say it aloud.

"And then somebody called Allman explored Vexvelt but—how did the report put it—'it was found on his return that Allman was suffering from confinement fatigue and his judgment was so severely impaired that his report is discounted.' Does that mean it was destroyed, Archive Master?"

Yes, thought the old man, but he said, "I can't say."

"So there you are," said Charli Bux. "If I wanted to present a classic case of what the old books called persecution mania, I'd just have to report things exactly as they happened. Did I have a right to suspect, even, that 'They' had picked me as the perfect target and set up those hints —low-cost feldspar, high-quality coffee—bait I couldn't miss and couldn't resist. Did I have the right to wonder if a living caricature with a comedy name—Moxie for-God's-sake Magiddle—was working for Them? Then, what happened next, when I honestly and openly filed for Vexvelt as my next vacation destination? I was told there was no Drive Guide orbiting Vexvelt—it could only be reached through normal space. That happens to be a lie, but there's no way of checking on it here, or even on Lethe—Moxie never knew. Then I filed for Vexvelt via Lethe and a real-space transport, and was told that Lethe was not recommended as a tourist stop and there was no real-space service from there anyhow. So I filed for Botil, which I *know* is a tourist stop, and which I know has real-space shuttles and charter boats, and which the star charts call Kricker III while Lethe is Kricker IV, and that's when I won the God—uh, the sweepstakes and a free trip to beautiful, beautiful Zeenip, paradise of paradises with two indoor thirty-six-hole golf courses and free milk baths. I gave it to some charity or other, I said to save on taxes, and went for my tickets to Botil, the way I'd planned. I had it all to do over because they'd wiped the whole transaction when they learned about the sweepstakes. It seemed reasonable but it took so long to set it all up again that I missed the scheduled transport and lost a week of my vacation. Then when I went to pay for the trip my credit showed up zero, and it took another week to straighten out that regrettable error. By that time the tour service had only one full passage open, and in view of the fact that the entire tour would outlast my vacation by two weeks, they wiped the whole deal again—they were quite sure I wouldn't want it."

Charli Bux looked down at his hands and squeezed them. The Archives Office was filled with a crunching sound. Bux did not seem to notice it. "I guess anybody in his right mind would have got the message by then, but 'They' had underestimated me. Let me tell you exactly what I mean by that. I *don't* mean that I am a man of steel and by the Lord when my mind is made up it stays made. And I'm not making brags about the courage of my convictions. I had very little to be convinced about, except that there was a whole chain of coincidences which nobody wanted to explain even though the explanation was probably foolishly simple. And I never thought I was specially courageous.

"I was just—scared. Oh, I was frustrated and I was mad, but mostly I was scared. If somebody had come along with a reasonable explanation I'd've forgotten the whole thing. If someone had come back from Vexvelt and it was a poison planet (with a pocket of good feldspar and one clean mountainside) I'd have laughed it off. But the whole sequence—especially the last part, trying to book passage—really scared me. I reached the point where the only thing that would satisfy me as to my own sanity was to stand and walk on Vexvelt and *know* what it was. And that was the one thing I wasn't being allowed to do. So I couldn't get my solid proof and who's to say I wouldn't spend the next couple hundred years wondering when I'd get the next little splinter down deep in my toe? A man can suffer from a thing, Master, but then he can also suffer for fear of suffering from a thing. No, I was scared and I was going to stay scared until I cleared it up."

"My." The old man had been silent, listening, for so long that his voice was new and arresting. "It seems to me that there was a much simpler way out. Every city on every human world has free clinics where—"

"That's twice you've said that," crackled Charli Bux. "I have something to say about that, but not now. As to my going to a patch-up parlor, you know as well as I do that they don't change a thing. They just make you feel good about being the way you are."

"I fail to see the distinction, or what is wrong if there is one."

"I had a friend come up to me and tell me he was going to die of cancer in the next eight weeks, 'just in time,' he says, and whacks me so hard I see red spots, 'just in time for my funeral,' and off he goes down the street whooping like a loon."

"Would it be better if he huddled in his bed terrified and in pain?"

"I can't answer that kind of a question, but I do know what I saw is just as wrong. Anyway—there was something out there called Vexvelt, and it wouldn't make me feel any better to get rolled through a machine and come out thinking there isn't something called Vexvelt, and don't tell me that's not what those friendly helpful spot removers would do to me."

"But don't you see, you'd no longer be—"

"Call me throwback. Call me radical if you want to, or ignorant." Charli Bux's big voice was up again and he seemed angry enough not to care. "Ever hear that old line about 'in every fat man there's a thin man screaming to get out'? I just can't shake the idea that if something is *so,* you can prick, poke and process me till I laugh and scratch and giggle and admit it ain't so after all, and even go out and make speeches and persuade other people, but away down deep there'll be a me with its mouth taped shut and its hands tied, bashing up against my guts trying to get out and say it is so after all. But what are we talking about me for? I came here to talk about Vexvelt."

"First tell me something—do you really think there was a 'They' who wanted to stop you?"

"*Hell* no. I think I'm up against some old-time stupidity that got itself established and habitual, and that's how come there's no information in the files. I don't think anybody today is all that stupid. I like to think people on this planet can look at the truth and not let it scare them. Even if it scares them they can think it through. As to that rat race with the vacation bookings, there seemed to be a good reason for each single thing that happened. Science and math have done a pretty good job of explaining the mechanics of 'the bad break' and 'a lucky run,' but neither one of them ever got repealed."

"So." The Master tented his fingers and looked down at the ridgepole. "And just how did you manage to get to Vexvelt after all?"

Bux flicked on his big bright grin. "I hear a lot about this free society, and how there's always someone out to trim an edge off here and a corner there. Maybe there's something in it, but so far they haven't got around to taking away a man's freedom to be a damn fool. Like, for example, his freedom to quit his job. I've said it was just a gruesome series of bad breaks, but bad breaks can be outwitted just as easily as a superpowerful masterminding 'They.' Seems to me most bad breaks happen inside a man's pattern. He gets out of phase with it and every step he takes is between the steppin'stones. If he can't phase in, and if he tries to maintain his pace, why there's a whole row of stones ahead of him laid just exactly where each and every one of them will crack his shins. What he should do is head upstream. It might be unknown territory, and there might be dangers, but one thing for sure, there's a whole row of absolutely certain, absolutely planned agonies he is just not going to have to suffer."

"How did you get to Vexvelt?"

"I told you." He waited, then smiled. "I'll tell you again. I quit my job. 'They,' or the 'losing streak,' or the stinking lousy Fates, or whatever had a bead on me—they could do it to me because they always knew where I was, when I'd be the next place, and what I wanted. So they were always waiting for me. So I headed upstream. I waited till my vacation was over and left the house without any luggage and went to my local bank and had all my credits before I could have any tough breaks.

Then I took a Drive jumper to Lunatu, booked passage on a semi-freight to Lethe."

"You booked passage, but you never boarded the ship."

"You know?"

"I was asking."

"Oh," said Charli Bux. "Yeah, I never set foot in that cozy little cabin. What I did, I slid down the cargo chute and got buried in Hold Number Two with a ton of oats. I was in an interesting position, Archive Master. In a way I'm sorry nobody dug me out to ask questions. You're not supposed to stow away but the law says—and I know exactly what it says—that a stowaway is someone who rides a vessel without booking passage. But I did book passage, and paid in full, and all my papers were in order for where I was going. What made things a lot easier, too, was that where I was going nobody gives much of a damn about papers."

"And you felt you could get to Vevxelt through Lethe."

"I felt I had a chance, and I knew of no other. Cargoes from Vexvelt *had* been put down on Lethe, or I wouldn't have been sucked into this thing in the first place. I didn't know if the carrier was Vexveltian or a tramp (if it was a liner I'd have known it) or when one might come or if it would be headed for Vexvelt when it departed. All I knew was that Vexvelt had shipped here for sure, and this was the only place where maybe they might be back. Do you know what goes on at Lethe?"

"It has a reputation."

"Do you *know?*"

The old man showed a twinge of irritation. Along with respect and obedience, he had become accustomed to catechizing and not to being catechized. "Everyone knows about Lethe."

Bux shook his head. "They don't, Master."

The old man lifted his hands and put them down.

"That kind of thing has its function. Humanity will al-ways—"

"You approve of Lethe and what goes on there."

"One neither approves nor disapproves," said the Archive Master stiffly. "One knows about it, recognizes that for some segments of the species such an outlet is necessary, realizes that Lethe makes no pretensions to being anything but what it is, and then—one accepts, one goes on to other things. How did you get to Vexvelt?"

"On Lethe," said Charli Bux implacably, "you can do anything you want to or with any kind of human being, or any number of combinations of them, as long as you can pay for it."

"I wouldn't doubt it. Now, the next leg of your trip—"

"There are men," said Charli Bux, suddenly and shock-ingly quiet, "who can be attracted by disease—by sores, Archive Master, by the stumps of amputated limbs. There are people on Lethe who cultivate diseases to attract such men. Crones, Master, with dirty leather skin, and boys and little—"

"You will cease this nauseating—"

"In just a minute. One of the unwritten and unbreak-able traditions of Lethe is that, what anyone pays to do, anyone else may pay to watch."

"Are you finished?" It was not Bux who shouted now.

"You accept Lethe. You condone Lethe."

"I have not said I approve."

"You trade with Lethe."

"Well, of course we do. That doesn't mean we—"

"The third day—night, rather, that I was there," said Bux, overriding what was surely about to turn into a help-less sputter, "I turned off one of the main streets into an alley. I knew this might be less than wise, but at the mo-ment there was an ugly fight going on between me and the corner, and some wild gunning. I was going to turn right and go to the other avenue anyway, and I could see it clearly through the alley.

"I couldn't describe to you how fast this happened, or explain where they came from—eight of them, I think, in an alley, not quite dark and very narrow, when only a minute before I had been able to see it from end to end.

"I was grabbed from all sides all over my body, lifted, slammed down flat on my back and a bright light jammed in my face.

"A woman said, 'Aw shoot, 'tain't him.' A man's voice said to let me up. They picked me up. Somebody even started dusting me off. The woman who had held the light began to apologize. She did it quite nicely. She said they had heard that there was a—Master, I wonder if I should use the word."

"How necessary do you feel—"

"Oh, I guess I don't have to; you know it. On any ship, any construction gang, in any farm community—anywhere where men work or gather, it's the one verbal bullet which will and must start a fight. If it doesn't, the victim will never regain face. The woman used it as casually as she would have said Terran or Lethean. She said there was one right here in town and they meant to get him. I said, 'Well, how about that.' It's the one phrase I know that can be said any time about anything. Another woman said I was a good big one and how would I like to tromp him. One of the men said all right, but he called for the head. Another began to fight him about it, and a third woman took off her shoe and slapped both their faces with one swing of the muddy sole. She said for them to button it up or next time she'd use the heel. The other woman, with the light, giggled and said Helen was Veddy Good Indeed that way. She spoke in a beautifully cultivated accent. She said Helen could hook out an eye neat as a croupier. The third woman suddenly cried out, 'Dog turds!' She asked for some light. The dog turds were very dry. One of the men offered to wet them down. The woman said no—they were her dog turds and she would do it herself. Then and there she squatted. She called for a light, said she couldn't see to aim. They turned the light on her. She was one of the most beautiful women I have ever seen. Is there something wrong, Master?"

"I would like you to tell me how you made contact with Vexvelt," said the old man a little breathlessly.

"But I am!" said Charli Bux. "One of the men pressed through, all grunting with eagerness, and began to mix the filth with his hands. And then, by a sort of sixth sense, the light was out and they were simply—*gone!* Disappeared. A hand came out of nowhere and pulled me back against a house wall. There wasn't a sound—not even breathing. And only then did the Vexveltian turn into the alley. How they knew he was coming is beyond me.

"The hand that had pulled me back belonged to the woman with the light, as I found out in a matter of seconds. I really didn't believe her hand meant to be where I found it. I took hold of it and held it, but she snatched it away and put it back. Then I felt the light bump my leg. And the man came along toward us. He was a big man, held himself straight, wore light-colored clothes, which I thought was more foolhardy than brave. He walked lightly and seemed to be looking everywhere—and still could not see us.

"If this all happened right this minute, after what I've learned about Vexvelt—about Lethe too—I wouldn't hesitate, I'd know exactly what to do. What you have to understand is that I didn't know anything at all at the time. Maybe it was the eight against one that annoyed me." He paused thoughtfully. "Maybe that coffee. What I'm trying to say is that I did the same thing then, in my ignorance, that I'd do now, knowing what I do.

"I snapped the flashlight out of the woman's hand and got about twenty feet away in two big bounds. I turned the

light on and played it back where I'd come from. Two of
the men had crawled up the sheer building face like insects and were ready to drop on the victim. The beautiful
one was crouched on her toes and one hand; the other,
full of filth, was ready to throw. She made an absolutely
animal sound and slung her handful, quite uselessly. The
others were flattened back against wall and fence, and in
the light, for a long second, they flattened all the more,
blinking. I said over my shoulder, 'Watch yourself, friend.
You're the guest of honor, I think.'

"You know what he did? He laughed. I said, 'They
won't get by me for a while. Take off.' 'What for?' says
he, squeezing past me. 'There's only eight of them.' And
he marches straight down on them.

"Something rolled under my foot and I picked it up—
half a brick. What must have been the other half of it
hit me right on the breastbone. It made me yelp, I couldn't
help it. The tall man said to douse the light, I was a target.
I did, and saw one of the men in silhouette against the
street at the far end, standing up from behind a big gar-
bage can. He was holding a knife half as long as his
forearm, and he rose up as the big man passed him. I let
fly with the brick and got him right back of the head. The
tall man never so much as turned when he heard him fall
and the knife go skittering. He passed one of the human
flies as if he had forgotten he was there, but he hadn't forgotten. He reached up and got both the ankles and swung
the whole man screaming off the wall like a flail, wiping
the second one off and tumbling the both of them on top
of the rest of the gang.

"He stood there with the back of his hands on his hips
for a bit, not even breathing hard, watching the crying,
cursing mix-up all over the alley pavement. I came up
beside him. One, two got to their feet and ran limping.
One of the women began to scream—curses, I suppose,

but you couldn't hear the words. I turned the light on her face and she shut right up.

" 'You all right?' says the tall man.

"I told him, 'Caved in my chest is all, but that's all right, I can use it for a fruit bowl lying in bed.' He laughed and turned his back on the enemy and led me the way he had come. He said he was Vorhidin from Vexvelt. I told him who I was. I said I'd been looking for a Vexveltian, but before we could go on with that a black hole opened up to the left and somebody whispered, 'Quick, quick.' Vorhidin clapped a hand on my back and gave me a little shove. 'In you go, Charli Bux of Terratu.' And in we went, me stumbling all over my feet down some steps I didn't know were there, and then again because they weren't there. A big door boomed closed behind us. Dim yellow light came on. There was a little man with olive skin and shiny, oily mustachios. 'Vorhidin, for the love of God, I told you not to come into town, they'll kill you.' Vorhidin only said, 'This is Charli Bux, a friend.' The little man came forward anxiously and began to pat Vorhidin on the arms and ribs to see if he was all right.

"Vorhidin laughed and brushed him off. 'Poor Tretti! He's always afraid something is going to happen! Never mind me, you fusspot. See to Charli here. He took a shot in the bows that was meant for me.' The little one, Tretti, sort of squeaked and before I could stop him he had my shirt open and the light out of my hand switched on and trained on the bruise. 'Your next woman can admire a sunset,' says Vorhidin. Tretti's away and back before you can blink and sprays on something cool and good and most of the pain vanished.

" 'What do you have for us?' and Tretti carries the light into another room. There's stacks of stuff, mostly manufactured goods, tools and instruments. There was a big pile of trideo cartridges, mostly music and new plays, but a novel or so too. Most of the other stuff was one of a kind. Vorhidin picked up a forty-pound crate and spun it twice by diagonal corners till it stopped where he could read the label. 'Molar spectroscope. Most of this stuff we don't really need but we like to see what's being done, how it's designed. Sometimes ours are better, sometimes not. We like to see, that's all.' He set it down gently and reached into his pocket and palmed out a dozen or more stones that flashed till it hurt. One of them, a blue one, made its own light. He took Tretti's hand and pulled it to him and poured it full of stones. 'That enough for this load?' I couldn't help it—I glanced around the place and totted it up and made a stab estimate—a hundred each of everything in the place wouldn't be worth that one blue stone. Tretti was goggle-eyed. He couldn't speak. Vorhidin wagged his head and laughed and said, 'All right, then,' and reached into his pants pocket again and ladled out four or five more. I thought Tretti was going to cry. I was right. He cried.

"We had something to eat and I told Vorhidin how I happened to be here. He said he'd better take me along. I said where to? and he said Vexvelt. I began to laugh. I told him I was busting my brains trying to figure some way to make him say that, and he laughed too and said I'd found it, all right, twice over. 'Owe you a favor for that,' he says, dipping his head at the alley side of the room. 'Reason two, you wouldn't live out the night on Lethe if you stayed here.' I wanted to know why not, because from what I'd seen there were fights all the time, then you'd see the fighters an hour later drinking out of the same bowl. He says it's not the same thing. Nobody helps a Vexveltian but a Vexveltian. Help one, you are one, far as Lethe was concerned. So I wanted to know what Lethe had against Vexvelt, and he stopped chewing and looked at me a long time as if he didn't understand me. Then he said, 'You really don't know anything about us, do you?' I said, not much. 'Well,' he says, 'now there's three good reasons to bring you.'

"Tretti opened the double doors at the far end of the storeroom. There was a ground van in there, with another set of doors into the street. We loaded the crates into it and got in, Vorhidin at the tiller. Tretti climbed a ladder and put his eyes to something and spun a wheel. 'Periscope,' Vorhidin told me. 'Looks like a flagpole from outside.' Tretti waved his hand at us. He had tears running down his cheeks again. He hit a switch and the doors banged out of the way. The van screeched out of there as the doors bounced and started back. After that Vorhidin drove like a little old lady. One-way glass. Sometimes I wondered what those crowds of drunks and queers would do if they could see in. I asked him, 'What are they afraid of?' He didn't seem to understand the question. I said, 'Mostly when people gang up on somebody, it's because one way or another they're afraid. What do they think you're going to take away from them?'

"He laughed and said, 'Their decency.' And that's all the talk I got out of him all the way out to the spaceport.

"The Vexveltian ship was parked miles away from the terminal, way the hell and gone at the far end of the pavement near some trees. There was a fire going near it. As we got closer I saw it wasn't near it, it was sprang under it. There was a big crowd, maybe half a hundred, mostly women, mostly drunk. They were dancing and staggering around and dragging wood up under the ship. The ship stood up on its tail like the old chemical rockets in the fairy stories. Vorhidin grunted, 'Idiots,' and moved something on his wrist. The rocket began to rumble and everybody ran screaming. Then there was a big explosion of steam and the wood went every which way, and for a while the pavement was full of people running and falling and screaming, and cycles and ground cars milling around and bumping each other. After a while it was quiet and we pulled up close. The high hatch opened on the ship and a boom and frame came out and lowered. Vorhidin hooked on, threw the latches on the van bed, beckoned me back there with him, reached forward and set the controls of the van, and touched the thing on his wrist. The whole van cargo section started up complete with us, and the van started up and began to roll home by itself.

"The only crew he carried," said Charli Bux carefully, "was a young radio officer." *With long shining black wings for hair and bits of sky in her tilted eyes, and a full and asking kind of mouth. She held Vorhidin very close, very long, laughing the message that there could be no words for this: he was safe.* "Tamba, this is Charli. He's from Terratu and he fought for me." *Then she came and held him too, and she kissed him; that incredible mouth, that warm, strong, soft mouth, why, he and she shared it for an hour; for an hour he felt her lips on his, even though she had kissed him for only a second. For an hour her lips could hardly be closer to her than they were to his own astonished flesh.* "The ship blasted off and headed sunward and to the celestial north. It held this course for two days. Lethe has two moons, the smaller one just a rock, an asteroid. Vorhidin matched velocities with it and hung half a kilo away, drifting in."

And the first night he had swung his bunk to the after bulkhead and had lain there heavily against the thrust of the jets, and against the thrust of his heart and his loins. Never had he seen such a woman—only just become woman, at that. So joyful, so utterly and so rightly herself. Half an hour after blastoff: "Clothes are in the way on ship, don't you think? But Vorhidin says I should ask you, because customs are different from one world to another, isn't that so?"

"Here we live by your customs, not mine," *Charli had been able to say, and she had thanked him, thanked him! and touched the bit of glitter at her throat, and her gar-*

*ment fell away. "There's much more privacy this way,"
she said, leaving him. "A closed door means more to the
naked; it's closed for a real reason and not because one
might be seen in one's petticoat." She took her garment into one of the staterooms. Vorhidin's. Charli leaned weakly against the bulkhead and shut his eyes. Her nipples were
like her mouth, full and asking. Vorhidin was casually
naked but Charli kept his clothes on, and the Vexveltians
made no comment. The night was very long. For a while
part of the weight on Charli turned to anger, which helped.
Old bastard, silver-temples. Old enough to be her father.
But that could not last, and he smiled at himself. He remembered the first time he had gone to a ski resort. There
were all kinds of people there, young, old, wealthy, working, professionals; but there was a difference. The resort,
because it was what it was, screened out the pasty-faced
the round-shouldered lungless sedentaries, the plumping
sybarites. All about him had been clear eyes, straight
backs, and skin with the cosmetics of frost and fun. Who
walked idled not, but went somewhere. Who sat lay back
joyfully in well-earned weariness. And this was the aura
of Vorhidin—not a matter of carriage and clean color and
clear eyes, though he certainly had all these, but the same
qualities down to the bone and radiating from the mind.
A difficult thing to express and a pleasure to be with.
Early on the second day Vorhidin had leaned close when
they were alone in the control room and asked him if he
would like to sleep with Tamba tonight. Charli gasped
as if he had been clapped on the navel with a handful of
crushed ice. He also blushed, saying, "If she, if she—"
wildly wondering how to ask her. He need not have wondered, for "He'd love to, honey," Vorhidin bellowed. Tamba popped her face into the corridor and smiled at Charli.
"Thank you so much," she said. And then (after the long
night) it was going to be the longest day he had ever lived
through, but she let it happen within the hour instead,*

sweetly, strongly, unhurried. Afterward he lay looking at her with such total and long-lasting astonishment that she laughed at him. She flooded his face with her black hair and then with her kisses and then all of him with her supple strength; this time she was fierce and most demanding until with a shout he toppled from the very peak of joy straight and instantly down into the most total slumber he had ever known. In perhaps twenty minutes he opened his eyes and found his gaze plunged deep in a blue glory, her eyes so close their lashes meshed. Later, talking to her in the wardroom, holding both her hands, he turned to find Vorhidin standing in the doorway. He was on them in one long stride, and flung an arm around each. Nothing was said. What could be said?

"I talked a lot with Vorhidin," Charli Bux said to the Archive Master. "I never met a man more sure of himself, what he wanted, what he liked, what he believed. The very first thing he said when I brought up the matter of trade was 'Why?' In all my waking life I never thought to ask that about trade. All I ever did, all anyone does, is to trade where he can and try to make it more. 'Why?' he wanted to know. I thought of the gemstones going for that production-line junk in the hold, and pure niobium at manganese prices. One trader would call that ignorance, another would call it good business and get all he could— glass beads for ivory. But cultures have been known to trade like that for religious or ethical reasons—always give more than you get in the other fellow's coin. Or maybe they were just—*rich*. Maybe there was so much Vexvelt that the only thing they could use was—well, like he said: manufacturers, so they could look at the design 'sometimes better than ours, sometimes not.' So I asked him.

"He gave me a long look that was, at four feet, exactly like" *drowning in the impossibly blue lakes of Tamba's eyes, but watch yourself, don't think about that when you talk to this old man* "holding still for an X-ray continuity.

Finally he said, 'Yes, I suppose we're rich. There's not much we need.'

"I told him, all the same, he could get a lot higher prices for the little he did trade. He just laughed a little and shook his head. 'You have to pay for what you get or it's no good. If you "trade well," as you call it, you finish with more than you started with; you didn't pay. That's as unnatural as energy levels going from lesser to greater, it's contrary to ecology and entropy.' Then he said, 'You don't understand that.' I didn't and I don't."

"Go on."

"They have their own Drive cradle back of Lethe's moon, and their own Guide orbiting Vexvelt. I told you— all the while I thought the planet was near Lethe; well, it isn't."

"Now, that I do *not* understand. Cradles and guides are public utilities. Two days, you say it took. Why didn't he use the one at the Lethe port?"

"I can't say, sir. Uh—"

"Well?"

"I was just thinking about that drunken mob building a fire under the ship."

"Ah yes. Perhaps the moon cradle is a wise precaution after all. I have always known, and you make it eminently clear, that these people are not popular. All right—you made a Drive jump."

"We made a Drive jump." Charli fell silent for a moment, reliving that breathless second of revelation as black, talc-dusted space and a lump moonlet winked away to be replaced by the great arch of a purple-haloed horizon, marbled green and gold and silver and polished blue, with a chromium glare coming from the sea on the planet's shoulder. "A tug was standing by and we got down without trouble." The spaceport was tiny compared even with Lethe—eight or ten docks, with the warehouse area under them and passenger and staff areas surrounding them under a deck. "There were no formalities—I suppose there's not enough space travel to merit them."

"Certainly no strangers, at any rate," said the old man smugly.

"We disembarked right on the deck and walked away." *Tamba had gone out first. It was sunny, with a warm wind, and if there was any significant difference between this gravity and that of Terratu, Charli's legs could not detect it. In the air, however, the difference was profound. Never before had he known air so clear, so winy, so clean—not unless it was bitter cold, and this was warm. Tamba stood by the silent, swiftly moving "up" ramp, looking out across the foothills to the most magnificent mountain range he had ever seen, for they had everything a picture-book mountain should have—smooth vivid high-range, shaggy forest, dramatic gray, brown, and ocher rock cliff, and a starched white cloth of snowcap tumbled on the peaks to dry in the sun. Behind them was a wide plain with a river for one margin and foothills for the other, and then the sea, with a wide golden beach curving a loving arm around the ocean's green shoulder. As he approached the pensive girl the warm wind curled and laughed down on them, and her short robe streamed from her shoulders like smoke, and fell about her again. It stopped his pace and his breath and his heart for a beat, it was so lovely a sight. And coming up beside her, watching the people below, the people rising on one ramp and sliding down the other, he realized that in this place clothing had but two conventions—ease and beauty. Man, woman, and child, they wore what they chose, ribbon or robe, clogs, coronets, cummerbunds or kilts, or a ring, or a snood, or nothing at all. He remembered a wonderful line he had read by a pre-Nova sage called Rudofsky, and murmured it:* Modesty is not so simple a virtue as honesty. *She turned and smiled at him; she thought it was his line. He smiled back and let her think so.* "You don't mind waiting *a bit? My father will be along in a moment and then we'll go. You're to stay with us. Is that all right?"*

Did he mind. Would he wait, bracketed by the thundering colors of that mountain, the adagio of the sea. Is that all right.

There was nothing, no way, no word to express his response but to raise his tense fists as high as he could and shout as loud as he could and then turn it into laughter and to tears.

Vorhidin, having checked out his manifests, joined them before Charli was finished. He had locked gazes with the girl, who smiled up at him and held his forearm in both her hands, stroking, and he laughed and laughed. "He drank too much Vexvelt all at once," she said to Vorhidin. Vorhidin put a big warm hand on Charli's shoulder and laughed with him until he was done. When he had his breath again, and the water-lenses out of his eyes, Tamba said, "That's where we're going."

"Where?"

She pointed, very carefully. Three slender dark trees like poplars came beseeching out of a glad tumble of luminous light willow-green. "Those three trees."

"I can't see a house . . "

Vorhidin and Tamba laughed together: this pleased them. "Come."

"We were going to wait for—"

"No need to wait any longer. Come."

Charli said, "The house was only a short walk from the port, but you couldn't see the one from the other. A big house, too, trees all around it and even growing up through it. I stayed with the family and worked." He slapped the heavy folio. "All this. I got all the help I needed."

"*Did* you indeed." The Archive Master seemed more interested in this than in anything else he had heard so far. Or perhaps it was a different kind of interest. "Helped you, did they? Would you say they're anxious to trade?"

The answer to this was clearly an important one. "All I can say," Charli Bux responded carefully, "is that I asked for this information—a catalogue of the trade resources of Vexvelt, and estimates of F.O.B. prices. None of them are very far off a practical, workable arrangement, and every single one undercuts the competition. There are a number of reasons. First of all, of course, is the resources themselves—almost right across the board, unbelievably rich. Then they have mining methods like nothing you've ever dreamed of, and harvesting, and preserving—there's no end to it. At first blush it looks like a pastoral planet— well, it's not. It's a natural treasure house that has been organized and worked and planned and understood like no other planet in the known universe. Those people have never had a war, they've never had to change their original cultural plan; it works, Master, it *works*. And it has produced a sane healthy people which, when it goes about a job, goes about it single-mindedly and with . . . well, it might sound like an odd term to use, but it's the only one that fits: with joy. . . . I can see you don't want to hear this."

The old man opened his eyes and looked directly at the visitor. At Bux's cascade of language he had averted his face, closed his eyes, curled his lip, let his hands stray over his temples and near his ears, as if it was taking a supreme effort to keep from clapping the palms over them.

"All I can hear is that a world which has been set aside by the whole species, and which has kept itself aloof, is using you to promote a contact which nobody wants. Do they want it? They won't get it, of course, but have they any idea of what their world would be like if this"—he waved at the folio—"is all true? How do they think they could control the exploiters? Have they got something special in defenses as well as all this other?"

"I really don't know."

"I know!" The old man was angrier than Bux had yet seen him. "What they are is their defense! No one will *ever* go near them, not *ever*. Not if they strip their whole planet of everything it has, and refine and process the lot, and haul it to their spaceport at their own expense, and give it away free."

"Not even if they can cure cancer?"

"Almost all cancer is curable."

"They can cure *all* cancer."

"New methods are discovered every—"

"They've had the methods for I don't know how many years. Centuries. *They have no cancer.*"

"Do you know what this cure is?"

"No, I don't. But it wouldn't take a clinical team a week to find out."

"The incurable cancers are not subject to clinical analysis. They are all deemed psychosomatic."

"I know. That is exactly what the clinical team would find out."

There was a long, pulsing silence. "You have not been completely frank with me, young man."

"That's right, sir."

Another silence. "The implication is that they are sane and cancer-free because of the kind of culture they have set up."

This time Bux did not respond, but let the old man's words hang there to be reheard, reread. At last the Archive Master spoke again in a near whisper, shaking and furious. "Abomination! Abomination!" Spittle appeared on his chin: he seemed not to know. "I would—rather—die— eaten alive—with cancer—and raving *mad* than live with such sanity as that."

"Perhaps others would disagree."

"No one would disagree! Try it? Try it! They'll tear you to pieces! That's what they did to Allman. That's what they did to Balrou! We killed Troshan ourselves—he was the first and we didn't know then that the mob would do it for us. That was a thousand years ago, you understand that? And a thousand years from now the mob will still do it for us! And that—that *filth* will go to the locked files with the others, and someday another fool with too much curiosity and not enough decency and his mind rotten with perversion will sit here with another Archive Master, who will send him out as I'm sending you out, to shut his mouth and save his life or open it and be torn to pieces. Get *out!* Get *out!* Get *out!*" His voice had risen to a shriek and then a sort of keening, and had rasped itself against itself until it was a painful forced whisper and then nothing at all: the old eyes glared and the chin was wet.

Charli Bux rose slowly. He was white with shock. He said quietly, "Vorhidin tried to tell me, and I wouldn't believe it. I couldn't believe it. I said to him, 'I know more about greed than you do; they will not be able to resist those prices.' I said, 'I know more about fear than you do; they will not be able to stand against the final cancer cure.' Vorhidin laughed at me and gave me all the help I needed.

"I started to tell him once that I knew more about the sanity that lives in all of us, and very much in some of us, and that it could prevail. But I knew while I was talking that I was wrong about that. Now I know that I was wrong in everything, even the greed, even the fear, and he was right. And he said Vexvelt has the most powerful and the least expensive defense ever devised—sanity. He was right."

Charli Bux realized then that the old man, madly locking gazes with him as he spoke, had in some way, inside his head, turned off his ears. He sat there with his old head cocked to one side, panting like a foundered dog in a dust bowl, until at last he thought he could shout again. He could not. He could only rasp, he could only whisper-squeak, "Get out! Get out!"

Charli Bux got out. He left the folio where it was; it, like Vexvelt, defended itself by being immiscible—in the language of chemistry, by being noble.

It was not Tamba after all, but Tyng who captured Charli's heart.

When they got to the beautiful house, so close to every-thing and yet so private, so secluded, he met the family. Breerho's radiant—almost heat-radiant—shining red hair, and Tyng's, showed them to be mother and daughter. Vor-hid and Stren were the sons, one a child, the other in his mid-teens, were straight-backed, wide-shouldered like their father, and by the wonderful cut and tilt of their architec-tured eyes, were brothers to Tyng, and to Tamba.

There were two other youngsters, a lovely twelve-year-old girl called Fleet, who was singing when they came in, and for whose song they stopped and postponed the in-troductions, and a sturdy tumblebug of a boy they called Handr, possibly the happiest human being any of them would ever see. In time Charli met the parents of these two, and black-haired Tamba seemed much more kin to the mother than to flame-haired Breerho.

It was a first a cascade of names and faces, captured only partially, kaleidoscoping about in his head as they all did in the room, and making a shyness in him. But there was more love in the room than ever the peaks of his mind and heart had known before, and more care and caring.

Before the afternoon and evening were over, he was familiar and accepted and enchanted. And because Tamba had touched his heart and astonished his body, all his feeling rose within him and narrowed and aimed them-selves on her, hot and breathless, and indeed she seemed to delight in him and kept close to him the whole time. But when the little ones went off yawning, and then others, and they were almost alone, he asked her, he begged her to come to his bed. She was kind as could be, and loving, but also completely firm in her refusal. "But, darling, I

just can't now. I can't. I've been away to Lethe and now
I'm back and I *promised*."

"Promised who?"

"Stren."

"But I thought . . ." He thought far too many things
to sort out or even to isolate one from another. Well, maybe he hadn't understood the relationships here—after all,
there were four adults and six children and he'd get it
straight by tomorrow who was who, because otherwise
she—oh. "You mean you promised Stren you wouldn't
sleep with me."

"No, my silly old dear. I'll sleep with Stren tonight.
Please, darling, don't be upset. There'll be other times.
Tomorrow. Tomorrow morning?" She laughed and took
his cheeks in her two hands and shook his whole head as
if she could make the frown drop off. "Tomorrow morning *very* early?"

"I don't mean to be like this my very first night here,
I'm sorry, I guess there's a lot I don't understand," he
mumbled in his misery. And then anguish skyrocketed
within him and he no longer cared about host and guest
and new customs and all the rest of it. "I love you," he
cried, "don't you know that?"

"Of course, of course I do. And I love you, and we will
love one another for a long, long time. Didn't you think I
knew that?" Her puzzlement was so genuine that even
through pain-haze he could see it. He said, as close to
tears as he felt a grown man should ever get, that he just
guessed he didn't understand.

"You will, beloved, you will. We'll talk about it until
you do, no matter how long it takes." Then she added,
with absolutely guileless cruelty, "Starting tomorrow. But
now I have to go, Stren's waiting. Good night, true love,"
and she kissed the top of his averted head and sprinted
away lightly on bare tiptoe.

She had reached something in him that made it impossible for him to be angry at her. He could only hurt. He had not known until these past two days that he could feel so much or bear so much pain. He buried his face in the cushions of the long couch in the—living room?—anyway, the place where indoors and outdoors were as tangled as his heart, but more harmoniously—and gave himself up to sodden hurt.

In time, someone knelt beside him and touched him lightly on the neck. He twisted his head enough to be able to see. It was Tyng, her hair all but luminous in the dimness, and her face, what he could see of it, nothing but compassion. She said, "Would you like me to stay with you instead?" and with the absolute honesty of the stricken he cried, "There couldn't be anyone else instead!"

Her sorrow, its genuineness, was unmistakable. She told him of it, touched him once more, and slipped away. Sometime during the night he twisted himself awake enough to find the room they had given him, and found surcease in utter black exhaustion.

Awake in daylight, he sought his other surcease, which was work and began his catalogue of resources. Everyone tried at one time or another to communicate with him, but unless it was work he shut it off (except, of course, for the irresistible Handr, who became his fast and lifelong friend). He found Tyng near him more and more frequently, and usefully so; he had not become so surly that he would refuse a stylus or reference book (opened at the right place) when it was placed in his hand exactly at the moment he needed it. Tyng was with him for many hours, alert but absolutely silent, before he unbent enough to ask her for this or that bit of information, or wondered about weights and measures and man-hour calculations done in the Vexveltian way. If she did not know, she found out with a minimum of delay and absolute clarity. She knew, however, a very great deal more than he had suspected. So the time came when he was chattering like a macaw, eagerly planning the next day's work with her.

He never spoke to Tamba. He did not mean to hurt her, but he could sense her eagerness to respond to him and he could not bear it. She, out of consideration, just stopped trying.

One particularly knotty statistical sequence kept him going for two days and two nights without stopping. Tyng kept up with him all the way without complaint until, in the wee small hours of the third morning, she rolled up her eyes and collapsed. He staggered up on legs gone asleep with too much sitting, and shook the statistics out of his eyes to settle her on the thick fur rug, straighten the twisted knee. In what little light spilled from his abandoned hooded lamp, she was exquisite, especially because of his previous knowledge that she was exquisite in the most brilliant of glares. The shadows added something to the alabaster, and her unconscious pale lips were no longer darker than her face, and she seemed strangely statuesque and nonliving. She was wearing a Cretan sort of dress, a tight stomacher holding the bare breasts cupped and supporting a diaphanous skirt. Troubled that the stomacher might impede her breathing, he unhooked it and put it back. The flesh of her midriff where it had been was, to the finger if not to the eye, pinched and ridged. He kneaded it gently and pursued indefinable thoughts through the haze of fatigue: pyrophyllite, Lethe, brother, recoverable vanadium salts, Vorhidin, precipitate, Tyng's watching me. Tyng in the almost dark was watching him. He took his eyes from her and looked down her body to his hand. It had stopped moving some vague time ago, slipped into slumber of its own accord. Were her eyes open now or closed? He leaned forward to see and over-balanced. They fell asleep with their lips touching, not yet having kissed at all.

The pre-Nova ancient Plato tells of the earliest human,

a quadruped with two sexes. And one terrible night in a
storm engendered by the forces of evil, all the humans
were torn in two; and ever since, each has sought the
other half of itself. Any two of opposite sexes can make
something, but it is usually incomplete in some way. But
when one part finds its true other half, no power on earth
can keep them apart, nor drive them apart once they join.
This happened that night, beginning at some moment so
deep in sleep that neither could ever remember it. What
happened to each was all the way into new places where
nothing had ever been before, and it was forever. The essence of such a thing is acceptance, and lest he be judged,
Charli Bux ceased to judge quite so much and began to
learn something of the ways of life around him. Life
around him certainly concealed very little. The children
slept where they chose. Their sexual play was certainly no
more enthusiastic or more frequent than any other kind of
play—and no more concealed. There was very much less
talk about sex than he had ever encountered in any group
of any age. He kept on working hard, but no longer to
conceal facts from himself. He saw a good many things he
had not permitted himself to see before, and found to his
surprise that they were not, after all, the end of the world.

He had one more very, very bad time coming to him.
He sometimes slept in Tyng's room, she sometimes in his.
Early one morning he awoke alone, recalling some elusive
part of the work, and got up and padded down to her
room. He realized when it was too late to ignore it what
the soft singing sound meant; it was very much later that
he was able to realize his fury at the discovery that this
special song was not his alone to evoke. He was in her
room before he could stop himself, and out again, shaking
and blind.

He was sitting on the wet earth in the green hollow under a willow when Vorhidin found him. (He never knew
how Vorhidin had accomplished this, nor for that matter

how he had come there himself.) He was staring straight ahead and had been doing so for so long that his eyeballs were dry and the agony was enjoyable. He had forced his fingers so hard down into the ground that they were buried to the wrists. Three nails were bent and broken over backwards and he was still pushing.

Vorhidin did not speak at all at first, but merely sat down beside him. He waited what he felt was long enough and then softly called the young man's name. Charli did not move. Vorhidin then put a hand on his shoulder and the result was extraordinary. Charli Bux moved nothing visibly but the cords of his throat and his jaw, but at the first touch of the Vexveltian's hand he threw up. It was what is called clinically "projectile" vomiting. Soaked and spattered from hips to feet, dry-eyed and staring, Charli sat still. Vorhidin, who understood what had happened and may even have expected it, also remained just as he was, a hand on the young man's shoulder. "Say the words!" he snapped.

Charli Bux swiveled his head to look at the big man. He screwed up his eyes and blinked them, and blinked again. He spat sour out of his mouth, and his lips twisted and trembled. "Say the words," said Vorhidin quietly but forcefully, because he knew Charli could not contain them but had vomited rather than enunciate them. "Say the words."

"Y-y—" Charli had to spit again. "You," he croaked. "You—her *father!*" he screamed, and in a split second he became a dervish, a windmill, a double flail, a howling wolverine. The loamy hands, blood-muddy, so lacked control from the excess of fury that they never became fists. Vorhidin crouched where he was and took it all. He did not attempt to defend himself beyond an occasional small accurate movement of the head, to protect his eyes. He could heal from almost anything the blows might do, but unless the blows were spent, Charli Bux might never heal at all. It went on for a long time because something in Charli would not show, probably would not even feel, fatigue. When the last of the resources was gone, the collapse was sudden and total. Vorhidin knelt grunting, got painfully to his feet, bent dripping blood over the unconscious Terran, lifted him in his arms, and carried him gently into the house.

Vorhidin explained it all, in time. It took a great deal of time, because Charli could accept nothing at all from anyone at first, and then nothing from Vorhidin, and after that, only small doses. Summarized from half a hundred conversations, this is the gist:

"Some unknown ancient once wrote," said Vorhidin, " ' 'Tain't what you don't know that hurts you; it's what you do know that ain't so.' Answer me some questions. Don't stop to think. (Now that's silly. Nobody off Vexvelt ever stops to think about incest. They'll say a lot, mind you, and fast, but they don't think.) I'll ask, you answer. How many bisexual species—birds, beasts, fish and insects included—how many show any sign of the incest taboo?"

"I really couldn't say. I don't recall reading about it, but then, who'd write such a thing? I'd say—quite a few. It would be only natural."

"Wrong. Wrong twice, as a matter of fact. *Homo sapiens* has the patent, Charli—all over the wall-to-wall universe, only mankind. Wrong the second: it would *not* be natural. It never was, it isn't, and it never will be natural."

"Matter of terms, isn't it? I'd call it natural. I mean, it comes naturally. It doesn't have to be learned."

"Wrong. It does have to be learned. I can document that, but that'll wait—you can go through the library later. Accept the point for the argument."

"For the argument, then."

"Thanks. What percentage of people do you think have sexual feelings about their siblings—brothers and sisters?"

"What age are you talking about?"

"Doesn't matter."

"Sexual feelings don't begin until a certain age, do they?"

"Don't they? What would you say the age is, on the average?"

"Oh—depends on the indi—but you did say 'average,' didn't you? Let's put it around eight. Nine maybe."

"Wrong. Wait till you have some of your own, you'll find out. I'd put it at two or three minutes. I'd be willing to bet it existed a whole lot before that, too. By some weeks."

"I don't believe it!"

"I know you don't," said Vorhidin. " 'Strue all the same. What about the parent of the opposite sex?"

"Now, that would have to wait for a stage of consciousness capable of knowing the difference."

"Wel-l-l—you're not as wrong as usual," he said, but he said it kindly. "But you'd be amazed at how early that can be. They can smell the difference long before they can see it. A few days, a week."

"I never knew."

"I don't doubt that a bit. Now, let's forget everything you've seen here. Let's pretend you're back on Lethe and I ask you, what would be the effects on a culture if each individual had immediate and welcome access to all the others?"

"*Sexual* access?" Charli made a laugh, a nervous sort of sound. "Sexual excess, I'd call it."

"There's no such thing," said the big man flatly. "Depending on who you are and what sex, you can do it only until you can't do it any more, or you can keep on until finally nothing happens. One man might get along beautifully with some mild kind of sexual relief twice a month or less. Another might normally look for it eight, nine times a day."

"I'd hardly call that normal."

"I would. Unusual it might be, but it's one hundred per-cent normal for the guy who has it, long as it isn't patho-logical. By which I mean, capacity is capacity, by the cupful, by the horsepower, by the flight ceiling. Man or machine, you do no harm by operating within the param-eters of design. What does do harm—lots of it, and some of the worst kind—is guilt and a sense of sin, where the sin turns out to be some sort of natural appetite. I've read case histories of boys who have suicided because of a noc-turnal emission, or because they yielded to the temptation to masturbate after five, six weeks of self-denial—a denial, of course, that all by itself makes them preoccupied, ab-solutely obsessed by something that should have no more importance than clearing the throat. (I wish I could say that this kind of horror story lives only in the ancient scripts, but on many a world right this minute, it still goes on.)

"This guilt and sin thing is easier for some people to understand if you take it outside the area of sex. There are some religious orthodoxies which require a very specific diet, and the absolute exclusion of certain items. Given enough indoctrination for long enough, you can keep a man eating only (we'll say) 'flim' while 'flam' is forbidden. He'll get along on thin moldy flim and live half-starved in a whole warehouse full of nice fresh flam. You can make him ill—even kill him, if you have the knack—just by convincing him that the flim he just ate was really flam in disguise. Or you can drive him psychotic by slipping him suggestions until he acquires a real taste for flam and gets a supply and hides it and nibbles at it secretly every time he fights temptation and loses.

"So imagine the power of guilt when it isn't a flim-and-flam kind of manufactured orthodoxy you're violating, but a deep pressure down in the cells somewhere. It's as mad, and as dangerous, as grafting in an ethical-guilt structure which forbids or inhibits yielding to the need for the B-vitamin complex or potassium."

"Oh, but," Charli interrupted, "now you're talking about vital necessities—survival factors."

"I sure as hell am," said Vorhidin in Charli's own idiom, and grinned a swift and hilarious—and very accurate—imitation of Charli's flash-beacon smile. "Now it's time to trot out some of the things I mentioned before, things that can hurt you much more than ignorance—the things you know that ain't so." He laughed suddenly. "This is kind of fun, you know? I've been to a lot of worlds, and some are miles and years different from others in a thousand ways: but this thing I'm about to demonstrate, this particular shut-the-eyes, shut-the-brains conversation you can get anywhere you go. Are you ready? Tell me, then: what's wrong with incest? I take it back —you know me. Don't tell me. Tell some stranger, some fume-sniffer or alcohol addict in a spaceport bar." He put out both hands, the fingers so shaped that one could all but see light glisten from the imaginary glass he held. He said in a slurred voice, "Shay, shtranger, whut's a-wrong wit' in-shest, hm?" He closed one eye and rolled the other toward Charli.

Charli stopped to think. "You mean, morally, or what?"

"Let's skip that whole segment. Right and wrong depend on too many things from one place to another, although I have some theories of my own. No—let's be sitting in this bar and agree that incest is just awful, and go on from there. What's really wrong with it?"

"You breed too close, you get faulty offspring. Idiots and dead babies without heads and all that."

"I knew it! I knew it!" crowed the big Vexveltian. "Isn't it wonderful? From the rocky depths of a Stone Age culture through the brocades and knee-breeches sort of grand opera civilizations all the way out to the computer technocracies, where they graft electrodes into their heads and shunt their thinking into a box—you ask that question and you get that answer. It's something everybody just *knows*. You don't have to look at the evidence."

"Where do you go for evidence?"

"To dinner, for one place, where you'll eat idiot pig or feeble-minded cow. Any livestock breeder will tell you that, once you have a strain you want to keep and develop, you breed father to daughter and to granddaughter, and then brother to sister. You keep that up indefinitely until the desirable trait shows up recessive, and you stop it there. But it might never show up recessive. In any case, it's rare indeed when anything goes wrong in the very first generation; but you in the bar, there, you're totally convinced that it will. And are you prepared to say that every mental retard is the product of an incestuous union? You'd better not, or you'll hurt the feelings of some pretty nice people. That's a tragedy that can happen to anybody, and I doubt there's any more chance of it between related parents than there is with anyone else.

"But you still don't see the funniest . . . or maybe it's just the oddest part of that thing you know that just ain't so. Sex is a pretty popular topic on most worlds. Almost every aspect of it that is ever mentioned has nothing to do with procreation. For every mention of pregnancy or childbirth, I'd say there are hundreds which deal only with the sex act itself. But mention incest, and the response always deals with offspring. Always! To consider and discuss a pleasure or love relationship between blood relatives, you've apparently got to make some sort of special mental effort that nobody, anywhere, seems able to do easily—some not at all."

"I have to admit I never made it. But then—what *is* wrong with incest, with or without pregnancy?"

"Aside from moral considerations, you mean. The moral consideration is that it's a horrifying thought, and it's a horrifying thought because it always has been.

Biologically speaking, I'd say there's nothing wrong with it. Nothing. I'd go even further, with Dr Phelvelt—ever hear of him?"

"I don't think so."

"He was a biological theorist who could get one of his books banned on worlds that had never censored anything before—even on worlds which had science and freedom of research and freedom of speech as the absolute keystones of their whole structure. Anyway, Phelvelt had a very special kind of mind, always ready to take the next step no matter where it is, without insisting that it's somewhere where it isn't. He thought well, he wrote well, and he had a vast amount of knowledge outside his specialty and a real knack for unearthing what he happened not to know. And he called that sexual tension between blood relatives a survival factor."

"How did he come to that?"

"By a lot of separate paths which came together in the same place. Everybody knows (this one *is* so!) that there are evolutionary pressures which make for changes in a species. Not much (before Phelvelt) had been written about stabilizing forces. But don't you see, inbreeding is one of them?"

"Not offhand, I don't."

"Well, look at it, man! Take a herd animal as a good example. The bull covers his cows, and when they deliver heifers and the heifers grow up, he covers them too. Sometimes there's a third and even fourth generation of them before he gets displaced by a younger bull. And all that while, the herd characteristics are purified and reinforced. You don't easily get animals with slightly different metabolisms which might tend to wander away from the feeding ground the others were using. You won't get high-bottom cows which would necessitate Himself bringing something to stand on when he came courting." Through Charli's shout of laughter he continued, "So there you have it—stabilization, purification, greater survival value—all resulting from the pressure to breed in."

"I see, I see. And the same thing would be true of lions or fish or tree toads, or—"

"Or any animal. A lot of things have been said about Nature, that she's implacable, cruel, wasteful and so on. I like to think she's—reasonable. I concede that she reaches that state cruelly, at times, and wastefully and all the rest. But she has a way of coming up with the pragmatic solution, the one that works. To build in a pressure which tends to standardize and purify a successful stage, and to call in the exogene, the infusion of fresh blood, only once in several generations—that seems to me most reasonable."

"More so," Charli said, "than what we've always done, when you look at it that way. Every generation a new exogene, the blood kept churned up, each new organism full of pressures which haven't had a chance with the environment."

"I suppose," said Vorhidin, "you could argue that the incest taboo is responsible for the restlessness that pulled mankind out of the caves, but that's a little too simplistic for me. I'd have preferred a mankind that moved a little more slowly, a little more certainly, and never fell back. I think the ritual exogamy that made inbreeding a crime and 'deceased wife's sister' a law against incest is responsible for another kind of restlessness."

He grew very serious. "There's a theory that certain normal habit patterns should be allowed to run their course. Take the sucking reflex, for example. It has been said that infants who have been weaned too early plague themselves all their lives with oral activity—chewing on straws, smoking intoxicants in pipes, drinking out of bottles by preference, nervously manipulating the lips, and so on. With that as an analogy, you may look again at the restlessness of mankind all through his history. Who but a gaggle of frustrates, never in their lives permitted all the ways of love within the family, could coin such a concept as 'motherland' and give their lives to it and for it? There's a great urge to love Father, and another to topple him. Hasn't humanity set up its beloved Fathers, its Big Brothers, loved and worshiped and given and died for them, rebelled and killed and replaced them? A lot of them richly deserved it, I concede, but it would have been better to have done it on its own merits and not because they were nudged by a deep-down, absolutely sexual tide of which they could not speak because they had learned that it was unspeakable.

"The same sort of currents flow within the family unit. So-called sibling rivalry is too well known to be described, and the frequency of bitter quarreling between siblings is, in most cultures and their literature, a sort of cliché. Only a very few psychologists have dared to put forward the obvious explanation that, more often than not, these frictions are inverted love feelings, well salted with horror and guilt. It's a pattern that makes conflict between siblings all but a certainty, and it's a problem which, once stated, describes its own solution. . . . Have you ever read Vexworth? No? You should—I think you'd find him fascinating. Ecologist; in his way quite as much of a giant as Phelvelt."

"Ecologist—that has something to do with life and environment, right?"

"Ecology has *everything* to do with life and environment; it studies them as reciprocals, as interacting and mutually controlling forces. It goes without saying that the main aim and purpose of any life form is optimum survival; but 'optimum survival' is a meaningless term without considering the environment in which it has to happen. As the environment changes, the organism has to change its ways and means, even its basic design. Human beings are notorious for changing their environment, and in most of our history in most places, we have made these changes without ecological considerations. This is disaster, every time. This is overpopulation, past the capabilities of producing food and shelter enough. This is the rape of irreplaceable natural resources. This is the contamination of water supplies. And it is also the twisting and thwarting of psychosexual needs in the emotional environment.

"Vexvelt was founded by those two, Charli—Phelvelt and Vexworth—and is named for them. As far as I know it is the only culture ever devised on ecological lines. Our sexual patterns derive from the ecological base and are really only a very small part of our structure. Yet for that one aspect of our lives, we are avoided and shunned and pretty much unmentionable."

It took a long time for Charli to be able to let these ideas in, and longer for him to winnow and absorb them. But all the while he lived surrounded by beauty and fulfillment, by people, young and old, who were capable of total concentration on art and learning and building and processing, people who gave to each other and to their land and air and water just a little more than they took. He finished his survey largely because he had started it; for a while he was uncertain of what he would do with it.

When at length he came to Vorhidin and said he wanted to stay on Vexvelt, the big man smiled, but he shook his head. "I know you want to, Charli—but do you?"

"I don't know what you mean." He looked out at the dark bole of one of the Vexveltian poplars; Tyng was there, like a flower, an orchid. "It's more than that," said Charli, "more than my wanting to be a Vexveltian. You need me."

"We love you," Vorhidin said simply. "But—need?"

"If I went back," said Charli Bux, "and Terratu got its hands on my survey, what do you think would become of Vexvelt?"

"You tell me."

"First Terratu would come to trade, and then others, and then others; and then they would fight each other, and fight you . . . you need someone here who knows this, really knows it, and who can deal with it when it starts. It will start, you know, even without my survey; sooner or later someone will be able to do what I did—a shipment of feldspar, a sheet of pure metal. They will destroy you."

"They will never come near us."

"You think not. Listen: no matter how the other worlds disapprove, there is one force greater: greed."

"Not in this case, Charli. And this is what I want you to be able to understand, all the way down to your cells. Unless you do, you can never live here. We are shunned, Charli. If you had been born here, that would not matter so much to you. If you throw in your lot with us, it would have to be a total commitment. But you should not make such a decision without understanding how completely you will be excluded from everything else you have ever known."

"What makes you think I don't know it now?"

"You say we need defending. You say other-world traders will exploit us. That only means you don't understand. Charli: listen to me. Go back to Terratu. Make the strongest presentation you can for trade with Vexvelt. See how they react. Then you'll know—then you can decide."

"And aren't you afraid I might be right, and because of me, Vexvelt will be robbed and murdered?"

And Vorhidin shook his big head, smiling, and said, "Not one bit, Charli Bux. Not one little bit."

So Charli went back, and saw (after a due delay) the Archive Master, and learned what he learned, and came out and looked about him at his home world and, through that, at all the worlds like it; and then he went to the secret place where the Vexveltian ship was moored, and it opened to him. Tyng was there, Tamba, and Vorhidin. Charli said, "Take me home."

In the last seconds before they took the Drive jump, and he could look through the port at the shining face of Terratu for the last time in his life, Charli said, "Why? Why? How did Human being come to hate this one thing so much that they would rather die insane and in agony than accept it? How did it happen, Vorhidin?"

"I don't know," said the Vexveltian.

Afterword:

And now you know what sort of a science fiction story this is, and perhaps something about science fiction stories that you didn't know before.

I have always been fascinated by the human mind's ability to think itself to a truth, and then to take that one step more (truly the basic secret of all human progress) and the inability of so many people to learn the trick. Case in point "We mean to get that filth off the newsstands and out of the bookstores." Ask why, and most such crusaders will simply point at the "filth" and wonder that you asked. But a few will take one step more: "Because youngsters might get their hands on it." That satisfies most, but ask: "And suppose they do?" a still smaller minority will think it through to: "Because it's bad for them." Ask again: "In what way is it bad for them?" and a handful can reach this: "It will arouse them." By now you've probably run out of crusaders, but if there are a couple left, ask them, "How does being aroused harm a child?" and if you can get them to take that one more step, they will have to take it out of the area of emotional conviction and into the area of scientific research. Such studies are available, and invariably they show that such arousement is quite harmless—indeed, there is something abnormal about anyone who is not or cannot be so aroused. The only possible harm that can result comes not from the sexual response itself but from the guilt-making and punitive attitude of the social environment—most of all that part of it which is doing the crusading.

Casting about for some more or less untouched area in which to exercise this one-step-more technique, I hit on this one. That was at least twenty years ago, and I have had to wait until now to find a welcome for anything so unsettling. I am, of course, very grateful. I hope the yarn starts some fruitful argument.

WHEN YOU CARE,
WHEN YOU LOVE

He was beautiful in her bed.

When you care, when you love, when you treasure someone, you can watch the beloved in sleep as you watch everything, anything else—laughter, lips to a cup, a look even away from you; a stride, sun a-struggle lost in a hair-lock, a jest or a gesture—even stillness, even sleep.

She leaned close, all but breathless, and watched his lashes. Now, lashes are thick sometimes, curled, russet; these were all these, and glossy besides. Look closely—there where they curve lives light in tiny serried scimitars.

All so good, so very good, she let herself deliciously doubt its reality. She would let herself believe, in a moment, that this was real, was true, was here, had at last happened. All the things her life before had ever given her, all she had ever wanted, each by each had come to her purely for wanting. Delight there might be, pride, pleasure, even glory in the new possession of gift, privilege, object, experience: her ring, hat, toy, trip to Trinidad; yet, with possession there had always been (until now) the platter called *well, of course* on which these things were served her. For had she not wanted it? But this, now—*him*, now . . . greatest of all her wants, ever; first thing in all her life to transcend want itself and knowingly become need: this she had at last, at long (how long, now) long last, this she had now for good and all, for always, forever and never a touch of *well, of course*. He was her personal miracle, he in this bed now, warm and loving her. He was the reason and the reward of it all—her family and forbears, known by so few and felt by so many, and indeed, the whole history of mankind leading up to it, and all she herself had been and done and felt; and loving him, and losing him, and seeing him dead and bringing him back—it was all for this moment and because the moment had to be, he and this peak, this warmth in these sheets, this *now* of hers. He was all life and all life's beauty, beautiful in her bed; and now she could be sure, could believe it, believe . . .

"I do," she breathed. "I do."

"What do you do?" he asked her. He had not moved, and did not now.

"Devil, I thought you were asleep."

"Well, I was. But I had the feeling someone was looking."

"Not looking," she said softly. "Watching." She was watching the lashes still, and did not see them stir, but between them now lay a shining sliver of the gray, cool aluminum of his surprising eyes. In a moment he would look at her—just that—in a moment their eyes would meet and it would be as if nothing new had happened (for it would be the same metal missile which had first impaled her) and also as if everything, everything were happening again. Within her, passion boiled up like a fusion fireball, so beautiful, so huge—

—and like the most dreaded thing on earth, without pause the radiance changed, shifting from the hues of all the kinds of love to all the tones of terror and the colors of a cataclysm.

She cried his name . . .

And the gray eyes opened wide in fear for her fears and in astonishment, and he bounded up laughing, and the curl of his laughing lips turned without pause to the

pale writhing of agony, and they shrank apart, too far
apart while the white teeth met and while between them
he shouted his hurt. He fell on his side and doubled up,
grunting, gasping in pain . . . grunting, gasping, wrapped
away from her, unreachable even by her.

She screamed. She screamed. She—

A Wyke biography is hard to come by. This has been
true for four generations, and more true with each, for
the more the Wyke holdings grew, the less visible have
been the Wyke family, for so Cap'n Gamaliel Wyke willed
it after his conscience conquered him. This (for he was a
prudent man) did not happen until after his retirement
from what was euphemistically called the molasses, to
Europe, having brought molasses from the West Indies to
New England. Of course a paying cargo was needed for
the westward crossing, to close with a third leg this prof-
itable triangle, and what better cargo than Africans for
the West Indies, to harvest the cane and work in the mills
which made the molasses?

Ultimately affluent and retired, he seemed content for
a time to live among his peers, carrying his broadcloth
coat and snowy linen as to the manor born, limiting his
personal adornment to a massive golden ring and small
square gold buckles at his knee. Soberly shop-talking molasses often, rum seldom, slaves never, he dwelt with a
frightened wife and a silent son, until she died and something—perhaps loneliness—coupled his brain again to his
sharp old eyes, and made him look about him. He began
to dislike the hypocrisy of man and was honest enough
to dislike himself as well, and this was a new thing for
the Cap'n; he could not deny it and he could not contain
it, so he left the boy with the household staff and, taking
only a manservant, went into the wilderness to search his
soul.

The wilderness was Martha's Vineyard, and right

through a bitter winter the old man crouched by the fire when the weather closed in, and, muffled in four great gray shawls, paced the beaches when it was bright, his brass telescope under his arm and his grim canny thoughts doing mighty battle with his convictions. In the late spring, he returned to Wiscassett, his blunt certainty regained, his laconic curtness increased almost to the point of speechlessness. He sold out (as a startled contemporary described it) "everything that showed," and took his son, an awed, obedient eleven, back to the Vineyard where, to the accompaniment of tolling breakers and creaking gulls, he gave the boy an education to which all the schooling of all the Wykes for all of four generations would be mere addenda.

For in his retreat to the storms and loneliness of the inner self and the Vineyard, Gamaliel Wyke had come to terms with nothing less than the Decalogue.

He had never questioned the Ten Commandments, nor had he knowingly disobeyed them. Like many another before him, he attributed the sad state of the world and the sin of its inhabitants to their refusal to heed those Rules. But in his ponderings, God Himself, he at last devoutly concluded, had underestimated the stupidity of mankind. So he undertook to amend the Decalogue himself, by adding ". . . or cause . . ." to each Commandment, just to make it easier for a man to work with:

". . . or cause the Name of the Lord to be taken in vain."

". . . or cause stealing to be done."

". . . or cause dishonor to thy father and thy mother."

". . . or cause the commission of adultery."

". . . or cause a killing to be done."

But his revelation came to him when he came to the last one. It was suddenly clear to him that all mankind's folly —all greed, lust, war, all dishonor, sprang from humanity's almost total disregard for this edict and its amendment: "Thou shalt not covet . . . *nor cause covetousness!*"

It came to him then that to arouse covetousness in another is just as deadly a sin as to kill him or to cause his murder. Yet all around the world empires rose, great yachts and castles and hanging gardens came into being, tombs and trusts and college grants, all for the purpose of arousing the envy or covetousness of the less endowed —or having that effect no matter what the motive.

Now, one way for a man as rich as Gamaliel Wyke to have resolved the matter for himself would be St. Francis' way; but (though he could not admit this, or even recognize it) he would have discarded the Decalogue and his amendments, all surrounding Scripture and his gnarled right arm rather than run so counter to his inborn, ingrained Yankee acquisitiveness. And another way might have been to take his riches and bury them in the sand of Martha's Vineyard, to keep them from causing covetousness; the very thought clogged his nostrils with the feel of dune-sand and he felt suffocation; to him money was a living thing and should not be interred.

And so he came to his ultimate answer: Make your money, enjoy it, but *never let anyone know.* Desire, he concluded, for a neighbor's wife, or a neighbor's ass, or for anything, presupposed knowing about these possessions. No neighbor could desire anything of his if he couldn't lay a name to it.

So Gamaliel brought weight like granite and force like gravity to bear upon the mind and soul of his son Walter, and Walter begat Jedediah, and Jedediah begat Caiaphas (who died) and Samuel, and Samuel began Zebulon (who died) and Sylva; so perhaps the true beginning of the story of the boy who became his own mother lies with Cap'n Gamaliel Wyke and his sand-scoured, sea-deep, rock-hard revelation.

—fell on his side on the bed and doubled up, grunting,

gasping, wrapped away from her, even her, unreachable even by her.

She screamed. She screamed. She pressed herself up and away from him and ran naked into the sitting room, pawed up the ivory telephone: "Keogh" she cried; "For the love of God, *Keogh!*"

—and back into the bedroom where he lay open-mouthing a grating horrible *uh uh!* while she wrung her hands, tried to take one of his, found it agony-tense and unaware of her. She called him, called him, and once, screamed again.

The buzzer sounded with inexcusable discretion.

"Keogh!" she shouted, and the polite buzzer *shhh'd* her again—the lock, oh the damned lock . . . she picked up her negligee and ran with it in her hand through the dressing room and the sitting room and the hall and the living room and the foyer and flung open the door. She pulled Keogh through it before he could turn away from her; she thrust one arm in a sleeve of the garment and shouted at him, "Keogh, please, please, Keogh, what's wrong with him?" and she fled to the bedroom, Keogh sprinting to keep up with her.

Then Keogh, chairman of the board of seven great corporations, board-member of a dozen more, general manager of a quiet family holding company which had, for most of a century, specialized in the ownership of corporate owners, went to the bed and fixed his cool blue gaze on the agonized figure there.

He shook his head slightly.

"You called the wrong man," he snapped, and ran back to the sitting-room, knocking the girl aside as if he had been a machine on tracks. He picked up the phone and said, "Get Rathburn up here. *Now.* Where's Weber? You don't? Well, find him and get him here. . . I don't care. Hire an airplane. *Buy* an airplane."

He slammed down the phone and ran back into the

bedroom. He came up behind her and gently lifted the negligee onto her other shoulder, and speaking gently to her all the while, reached round her and tied the ribbon belt. "What happened?"

"N-nothing, he just—"

"Come on, girl—clear out of here. Rathburn's practically outside the door, and I've sent for Weber. If there's a better doctor than Rathburn, it could only be Weber, so you've got to leave it to them. Come!"

"I won't leave him."

"Come!" Keogh rapped; then murmured, looking over her shoulder at the bed, "He wants you to, can't you see? He doesn't want you to see him like this. *Right?*" he demanded, and the face, turned away and half-buried in the pillow shone sweatly; cramp mounded the muscles on the side of the mouth they could just see. Stiffly the head nodded; it was like a shudder. "And . . . shut . . . door . . . tight . . . ," he said in a clanging half whisper.

"Come," said Keogh. And again, "Come." He propelled her away; she stumbled. Her face turned yearningly until Keogh, both hands on her, kicked at the door and it swung and the sight of the bed was gone. Keogh leaned back against the door as if the latch were not enough to hold it closed.

"What is it? Oh, what is it?"

"I don't know," he said.

"You do, you do . . . you always know everything . . . why won't you let me stay with him?"

"He doesn't want that."

Overcome, inarticulate, she cried out.

"Maybe," he said into her hair, "he wants to scream too."

She struggled—oh, strong, lithe and strong she was. She tried to press past him. He would not budge, so at last, at last she wept.

He held her in his arms again, as he had not done since

she used to sit on his lap as a little girl. He held her in his arms and looked blindly toward the unconcerned bright morning, seen soft-focused through the cloud of her hair. And he tried to make it stop, the morning, the sun, and time, but—

—but there is one certain thing only about a human mind, and that is that it acts, moves, works ceaselessly while it lives. The action, motion, labor differ from that of a heart, say, or an epithelial cell, in that the latter have functions, and in any circumstance perform their functions. Instead of a function, mind has a duty, that of making of a hairless ape a human being . . . yet as if to prove how trivial a difference there is between mind and muscle, mind must move, to some degree, always change, to some degree, always while it lives, like a stinking sweat gland . . . holding her, Keogh thought about Keogh.

The biography of Keogh is somewhat harder to come by than that of a Wyke. This is not in spite of having spent merely half a lifetime in this moneyed shadow; it is because of it. Keogh was a Wyke in all but blood and breeding: Wyke owned him and all he owned, which was a great deal.

He must have been a child once, a youth; he could remember if he wished but did not care to. Life began for him with the *summa cum laude,* the degrees in both business and law and (so young) the year and a half with Hinnegan and Bache, and then the incredible opening at the International Bank; the impossible asked of him in the Zurich-Plenum affair, and his performance of it, and the shadows which grew between him and his associates over the years, while for him the light grew and grew as to the architecture of his work, until at last he was admitted to Wyke, and was permitted to realize that Wyke *was* Zurich and Plenum, and the International Bank, and Hinnegan and Bache; was indeed his law school and his college and much, so very much more. And finally sixteen—good heavens, it was eighteen years ago, when he became General Manager, and the shadows dark to totally black between him and any other world, while the light, his own huge personal illumination, exposed almost to him alone an industrial-financial complex unprecedented in his country, and virtually unmatched in the world.

But then, the beginning, the *other* beginning, was when Old Sam Wyke called him in so abruptly that morning, when (though General Manager with many a board chairman, all unbeknownst, under him in rank) he was still the youngest man in that secluded office.

"Keogh," said old Sam, "this is my kid. Take 'er out. Give 'er anything she wants. Be back here at six." He had then kissed the girl on the crown of her dark straw hat, gone to the door, turned and barked, "You see her show off or brag, Keogh, you fetch her a good one, then and there, hear? I don't care what else she does, but don't you let her wave something she's got at someone that hasn't got it. That's Rule One." He had then breezed out, leaving a silent, startled young mover of mountains locking gazes with an unmoving mouse of an eleven-year-old girl. She had luminous pale skin, blue-black silky-shining hair, and thick, level, black brows.

The *summa cum laude*, the acceptance at Hinnegan and Bache—all such things, they were beginnings that he knew were beginnings. This he would not know for some time that it was a beginning, any more than he could realize that he had just heard the contemporary version of Cap'n Gamaliel's "Thou shalt not . . . cause covetousness." At the moment, he could only stand nonplussed for a moment, then excuse himself and go to the treasurer's office, where he scribbled a receipt and relieved the petty cash box of its by no means petty contents. He got his hat and coat and returned to the President's office. Without a word the child rose and moved with him to the door.

They lunched and spent the afternoon together, and

were back at six. He bought her whatever she wanted at one of the most expensive shops in New York. He took her to just the places of amusement she asked him to.

When it was tall over, he returned the stack of bills to the petty cash box, less the one dollar and twenty cents he had paid out. For at the shop—the largest toy store in the world—she had carefully selected a sponge rubber ball, which they packed for her in a cubical box. This she carried carefully by its string for the rest of the afternoon.

They lunched from a pushcart—he had one hot dog with kraut, she had two with relish.

They rode uptown on the top of a Fifth Avenue double-decker, open-top bus.

They went to the zoo in Central Park and bought one bag of peanuts for the girl and the pigeons, and one bag of buns for the girl and the bears.

Then they took another double-decker back downtown, and that was it; that was the afternoon.

He remembered clearly what she looked like then: like a straw-hatted wren, for all it was a well-brushed wren. He could not remember what they had talked about, if indeed they had talked much at all. He was prepared to forget the episode, or at least to put it neatly in the *Trivia: Misc.: Closed* file in his compartmented mind, when, a week later, old Sam tossed him a stack of papers and told him to read them through and come and ask questions if he thought he had to. The only question which came to mind when he had read them was, "Are you sure you want to go through with this?" and that was not the kind of question one asked old Sam. So he thought it over very carefully and came up with "Why me?" and old Sam looked him up and down and growled, "She likes you, that's why."

And so it was that Keogh and the girl lived together in a cotton mill town in the South for a year. Keogh worked in the company store. The girl worked in the mill; twelve-year-old girls worked in cotton mills in the South in those days. She worked the morning shift and half the evening shift, and had three hours' school in the afternoons. Up until ten o'clock on Saturday nights they watched the dancing from the sidelines. On Sundays they went to the Baptist church. Their name while they were there was Harris. Keogh used to worry frantically when she was out of his sight, but one day when she was crossing the cat-walk over the water-circulating sump, a sort of oversized well beside the mill, the catwalk broke and pitched her into the water. Before she could so much as draw a breath a Negro stoker appeared out of nowhere—actually, out of the top of the coal chute—and leapt in and had her and handed her up to the sudden crowd. Keogh came galloping up from the company store as they were pulling the stoker out, and after seeing that girl was all right, knelt beside the man, whose leg was broken.

"I'm Mr. Harris, her father. You'll get a reward for this. What's your name?"

The man beckoned him close, and as he bent down, the stoker, in spite of his pain, grinned and winked. "You don' owe me a thang, Mr. Keogh," he murmured. In later times, Keogh would be filled with rage at such a con-fidence, would fire the man out of hand: this first time he was filled with wonder and relief. After that, things were easier on him, as he realized that the child was surrounded by Wyke's special employees, working on Wyke land in a Wyke mill and paying rent in a Wyke row-house.

In due time the year was up. Someone else took over, and the girl, now named Kevin and with a complete new background in case anyone should ask, went off for two years to a very exclusive Swiss finishing school, where she dutifully wrote letters to a Mr. and Mrs. Kevin who held large acreage in the Pennsylvania mountains, and who just as dutifully answered her.

Keogh returned to his own work, which he found in

apple-pie order, with every one of the year's transactions beautifully abstracted for him, and an extra amount, over and above his astronomical salary, tucked away in one of his accounts—an amount that startled even Keogh. He missed her at first, which he expected. But he missed her every single day for two solid years, a disturbance he could not explain, did not examine, and discussed with no one.

All the Wykes, old Sam once grunted to him, did something of the sort. He, Sam, had been a logger in Oregon and a year and a half as utility man, then ordinary seaman on a coastwise tanker.

Perhaps some deep buried part of Keogh's mind thought that when she returned from Switzerland, they would go for catfish in an old flat-bottomed boat again, or that she would sit on his lap while he suffered on the hard benches of the once-a-month picture show. The instant he saw her on her return from Switzerland, he knew that would never be. He knew he was entering some new phase; it troubled and distressed him and he put it away in the dark inside himself; he could do that; he was strong enough. And she —well, she flung her arms around him and kissed him; but when she talked with this new vocabulary, this deft school finish, she was strange and awesome to him, like an angel. Even a loving angel is strange and awesome . . .

They were together again then for a long while, but there were no more hugs. He became a Mr. Stark in the Cleveland office of a brokerage house and she boarded with an elderly couple, went to the local high school and had a part-time job filing in his office. This was when she learned the ins and outs of the business, the size of it. It would be hers. It became hers while they were in Cleveland: old Sam died very suddenly. They slipped away to the funeral but were back at work on Monday. They stayed there for another eight months; she had a great deal to learn. In the fall she entered a small private college and Keogh saw nothing of her for a year.

"Shhh," he breathed to her, crying, and *sssh!* said the buzzer.

"The doctor . . ."

"Go take a bath," he said. He pushed her.

She half-turned under his hand, faced him again blazing. "No!"

"You can't go in there, you know," he said, going for the door. She glared at him, but her lower lip trembled.

Keogh opened the door. "In the bedroom."

"Who—" then the doctor saw the girl, her hands knotted together, her face twisted, and had his answer. He was a tall man, gray, with quick hands, a quick step, swift words. He went straight through foyer, hall and rooms and into the bedroom. He closed the door behind him. There had been no discussion, no request and refusal; Dr. Rathburn had simply, quickly, quietly shut them out.

"Go take a bath."

"No."

"Come on." He took her wrist and led her to the bathroom. He reached into the shower stall and turned on the side jets. There were four at each corner; the second from the top was scented. Apple blossom. "Go on."

He moved toward the door. She stood where he had let go of her wrist, pulling at her hands. "Go on," he said again. "Just a quick one. Do you good." He waited. "Or do you want me to douse you myself? I bet I still can."

She flashed him a look; indignation passed instantly as she understood what he was trying to do. The rare spark of mischief appeared in her eyes and, in perfect imitation of a mill-row redneck, she said, "Y'all try it an Ah'll tall th' shurff Ah ain't rightly yo' chile." But the effort cost her too much, and she cried again. He stepped out and softly closed the door.

He was waiting by the bedroom when Rathburn slid out and quickly shut the door on the grunt, the gasp.

"What is it?" asked Keogh.

"Wait a minute." Rathburn strode to the phone. Keogh said, "I sent for Weber."

Rathburn came almost ludicrously to a halt. "Wow," he said. "Not bad diagnosing, for a layman. Is there anything you can't do?"

"I can't understand what you're talking about," said Keogh testily.

"Oh—I thought you knew. Yes, I'm afraid it's in Weber's field. What made you guess?"

Keogh shuddered. "I saw a mill hand take a low blow once. I know *he* wasn't hit. What exactly is it?"

Rathburn darted a look around. "Where is she?" Keogh indicated the bathroom. "I told her to take a shower."

"Good," said the doctor. He lowered his voice. "Naturally I can't tell without further examination and lab—"

"What is it?" Keogh demanded, not loud, but with such violence that Rathburn stepped back a pace.

"It could be choriocarcinoma."

Tiredly, Keogh wagged his head. "Me diagnose that? I can't even spell it. What is it?" He caught himself up, as if he had retrieved the word from thin air and run it past him again. "I know what the last part of it means."

"One of the—" Rathburn swallowed, and tried again. "One of the more vicious forms of cancer. And it . . ." He lowered his voice again. "It doesn't always hit this hard."

"Just how serious is it?"

Rathburn raised his hands and let them fall.

"Bad, eh? Doc—*how bad?*". .

"Maybe some day we can . . ." Rathburn's lowered voice at last disappeared. They hung there, each on the other's pained gaze.

"How much time?"

"Maybe six weeks."

"Six weeks!"

"Shh," said Rathburn nervously.

"Weber—"

"Weber knows more about internal physiology than anybody. But I don't know if that will help. It's a little like . . . your, uh, house is struck by lightning, flattened, burned to the ground. You can examine it and the weather reports and, uh, know exactly what happened. Maybe some day we can . . ." he said again, but he said it so hopelessly that Keogh, through the rolling mists of his own terror, pitied him and half-instinctively put out a hand. He touched the doctor's sleeve and stood awkwardly.

"What are you going to do?"

Rathburn looked at the closed bedroom door. "What I did." He made a gesture with a thumb and two fingers.

"Morphine."

"And that's all?"

"Look, I'm a G.P. Ask Weber, will you?"

Keogh realized that he had pushed the man as far as he could in his search for a crumb of hope; if there was none, there was no point in trying to squeeze it out. He asked, "Is there anyone working on it? Anything new? Can you find out?"

"Oh, I will, I will. But Weber can tell you off the top of his head more than I could find out in six mon . . . in a long time."

A door opened. She came out, hollow-eyed, but pink and glowing in a long white terry-cloth robe. "Dr. Rathburn—"

"He's asleep."

"Thank God. Does it—"

"There's no pain."

"What is it? What happened to him?"

"Well, I wouldn't like to say for sure . . . we're wating for Dr. Weber. He'll know."

"But—but is he—"

"He'll sleep the clock around."

"Can I . . ." The timidity, the caution, Keogh realized, was so unlike her. "Can I see him?"

"He's fast asleep!"

"I don't care. I'll be quiet. I won't—touch him or anything."

"Go ahead," said Rathburn. She opened the bedroom door and eagerly, silently slipped inside.

"You'd think she was trying to make sure he was there." Keogh, who knew her so very well, said, "She is."

But a biography of Guy Gibbon is *really* hard to come by. For he was no exceptional executive, who for all his guarded anonymity wielded so much power that he must be traceable by those who knew where to look and what to look for, and cared enough to process detail like a mass spectroscope. Neither was Guy Gibbon born heir to countless millions, the direct successor to a procession of giants.

He came from wherever it is most of us come from, the middle or the upper-middle, or the upper-lower middle or the lower-upper middle, or some other indefinable speck in the mid-range of the interflowing striations of society (the more they are studied, the less they mean). He belonged to the Wykes entity for only eight and a half weeks, after all. Oh, the bare details might not be too hard to come by—(birth date, school record) and certain main facts—(father's occupation, mother's maiden name)—as well, perhaps as a highlight or two—(divorce, perhaps, or a death in the family); but a biography, a real biography, which does more than describe, which *explains* the man— and few do—now, *this* is an undertaking.

Science, it is fair to assume, can do what all the king's horses and all the king's men could not do, and totally restore a smashed egg. Given equipment enough, and time enough . . . but isn't this a way of saying, "given money enough?" For money can be not only means, but motive. So if enough money went into the project, perhaps the last unknown, the last vestige of anonymity could be removed from a man's life story, even a young man from (as the snobs say) nowhere, no matter how briefly—though intimately—known.

The most important thing, obviously, that ever happened to Guy Gibbon in his life was his first encounter with the Wyke entity, and like many a person before and since, he had not the faintest idea he had done so. It was when he was in his late teens, and he and Sammy Stein went trespassing.

Sammy was a school sidekick, and this particular day he had a secret; he had been very insistent on the day's outing, but refused to say why. He was a burly-shouldered, good-natured, reasonably chinless boy whose close friendship with Guy was based almost exclusively on the attraction of opposite poles. And since, of the many kinds of fun they had had, the most fun was going trespassing, he wanted it that way on this particular occasion.

"Going trespassing," as an amusement, had more or less invented itself when they were in their early teens. They lived in a large city surrounded (unlike many today) by old suburbs, not new ones. These included large—some, more than large—estates and mansions, and it was their greatest delight to slip through a fence or over a wall and, profoundly impressed by their own bravery, slip through field and forest, lawn and drive, like Indian scouts in settler country. Twice they had been caught, once to have dogs set on them—three boxers and two mastiffs, which certainly would have torn them to very small pieces if the boys had not been more lucky than swift—and once by a dear little old lady who swamped them sickeningly with jelly sandwiches and lonely affection. But over the saga of their adventures, their two captures served to spice the adventure; two failures out of a hundred successes (for many of these places were visited frequently) was a proud record.

So they took a trolley to the end of the line, and walked a mile, and went straight ahead where the road turned at a discreet *No Admittance* sign of expensive manufacture and a high degree of weathering. They proceeded through a small wild wood, and came at last to an apparently unscalable granite wall.

Sammy had discovered this wall the week before, roaming alone; he had waited for Guy to accompany him before challenging it, and Guy was touched. He was also profoundly excited by the wall itself. Anything this size should have been found, conjectured about, campaigned against, battled and conquered long since. But as well as being a high wall, a long wall, and mysterious, it was a distant wall, a discreet wall. No road touched it but its own driveway, which was primitive, meandering, and led to ironbound, solid oak gates without a chink or crack to peek through.

They could not climb it nor breach it—but they crossed it. An ancient maple on this side held hands with a chestnut over the crown of the wall, and they went over like a couple of squirrels.

They had, in their ghost-like way, haunted many an elaborate property, but never had they seen such maintenance, such manicure, such polish of a piece of land and, as Sammy said, awed out of his usual brashness, as they stood in a solid marble pergola overlooking green plush acres of rolling lawn, copses of carven boxwood, park-like woods and streams with little Japanese bridges and, in their bends, humorful little rock-gardens: "—and there's goddam *miles* of it."

They had wandered a bit, that first time, and had learned that there were after all some people there. They saw a tractor far away, pulling a slanted gang of mowers across one of the green-plush fields. (The owners doubtless called it a lawn; it was a field.) The machines, rare in that time, cut a swath all of thirty feet wide, "and that," Sammy said, convulsing them, "ain't hay." And then they had seen the house—

Well, a glimpse. Breaking out of the woods, Guy had felt himself snatched back. "House up there," said Sammy. "Someone'll see us." There was a confused impression of a white hill that was itself the house, or part of it; towers, turrets, castellations, crenellations; a fairy-tale palace set in this legendary landscape. They had not been able to see it again; it was so placed that it could be approached nowhere secretly nor even spied upon. They were struck literally speechless by the sight and for most of an hour had nothing to say, and that expressible only by wags of the head. Ultimately they referred to it as "the shack," and it was in this vein that they later called their final discovery "the ol' swimmin' hole."

It was across a creek and over a wooded hill. Two more hills rose to meet the wood, and cupped between the three was a pond, perhaps a lake. It was roughly L-shaped, and all around it were shadowed inlets, grottoes, inconspicuous stone steps leading here to a rustic pavilion set about with flowers, there to a concealed forest glade harboring a tiny formal garden.

But the lake, the ol' swimmin' hole . . .

They went swimming, splashing as little as possible and sticking to the shore. They explored two inlets to the right (a miniature waterfall and a tiny beach of obviously imported golden sand) and three to the left (a square-cut one, lined with tile the color of patina, with a black glass diving tower overhanging water that must have been dredged to twenty feet; a little beach of snow-white sand; and one they dared not enter, for fear of harming the fleet of perfect sailing ships, none more than a foot long, which lay at anchor; but they trod water until they were bone-cold, gawking at the miniature model waterfront with little pushcarts in the street, and lamp-posts, and old-fashioned houses) and then, weary, hungry and awestruck, they had gone home.

And Sammy cracked the secret he had been keeping—the thing which made this day an occasion: he was to go wild-hairing off the next day in an effort to join Chennault in China.

Guy Gibbon, overwhelmed, made the only gesture he could think of: he devotedly swore he would not go trespassing again until Sammy got back.

"Death from choriocarcinoma," Dr. Weber began, "is the result of—"

"But he won't die," she said. "I won't let him."

"My dear," Dr. Weber was a small man with round shoulders and a hawk's face. "I don't mean to be unkind, but I can use all the euphemisms and kindle all the false hope, or I can do as you have asked me to do—explain the condition and make a prognosis. I can't do both."

Dr. Rathburn said gently, "Why don't you go and lie down? I'll come when we've finished here and tell you all about it."

"I don't want to lie down," she said fiercely. "And I wasn't asking you to spare me anything, Dr. Weber. I simply said I would not let him die. There's nothing in that statement which keeps you from telling me the truth."

Keogh smiled. Weber caught him at it and was startled; Keogh saw his surprise. "I know her better than you do," he said, with a touch of pride. "You don't have to pull any punches."

"Thanks, Keogh," she said. She leaned forward. "Go ahead, Dr. Weber."

Weber looked at her. Snatched from his work two thousand miles away, brought to a place he had never known existed, of a magnificence which attacked his confidence in his own eyes, meeting a woman of power—

every sort of power—quite beyond his experience . . . Weber had thought himself beyond astonishment. Shock, grief, fear, deprivation like hers he had seen before, of course; what doctor has not? but when Keogh had told her baldly that this disease killed in six weeks, *always,* she had flinched, closed her eyes for an interminable moment, and had then said softly, "Tell us everything you can about this—this disease, Doctor." And she had added, for the first time, "He isn't going to die. I won't let him"; and the way she held her head, the way her full voice handled the words, he almost believed her. Heaven knows, he wished he could. And so he found he could be astonished yet again.

He made an effort to detach himself, and became not a man, not this particular patient's doctor, but a sort of source-book. He began again:

"Death from choriocarcinoma is a little unlike other deaths from malignancies. Ordinarily a cancer begins locally, and sends its chains and masses of wild cells growing through the organ on which it began. Death can result from the failure of that organ; liver, kidney, brain, what have you. Or the cancer suddenly breaks up and spreads through the body, starting colonies throughout the system. This is called metastasis. Death results then from the loss of efficiency of many organs instead of just one. Of course, both these things can happen—the almost complete impairment of the originally cancerous organ, and metastatic effects at the same time.

"Chorio, on the other hand, doesn't originally involve a vital organ. Vital to the species, perhaps, but not to the individual." He permitted himself a dry smile. "This is probably a startling concept to most people in this day and age, but it's nonetheless true. However, sex cells, at their most basic and primitive, have peculiarities not shared by other body cells.

"Have you ever heard of the condition known as

ectopic pregnancy?" He directed his question at Keogh, who nodded. "A fertilized ovum fails to descend to the uterus; instead it attaches itself to the side of the very fine tube between the ovaries and the womb. And at first everything proceeds well with it—and this is the point I want you to grasp—because in spite of the fact that only the uterus is truly specialized for this work, the tube wall not only supports the growing ovum but feeds it. It actually forms what we call a counterplacenta; it enfolds the early fetus and nurtures it. The fetus, of course, has a high survival value, and is able to get along quite well on the plasma which the counterplacenta supplies it with. And it grows—it grows fantastically. Since the tube is very fine—you'd have difficulty getting the smallest needle up through it—it can no longer contain the growing fetus, and ruptures. Unless it is removed at that time, the tissues outside will quite as readily take on the work of a real placenta and uterus, and in six or seven months, if the mother survives that long, will create havoc in the abdomen.

"All right then: back to chorio. Since the cells involved are sex cells, and cancerous to boot, they divide and re-divide wildly, without pattern or special form. They develop in an infinite variety of shapes and sizes and forms. The law of averages dictates that a certain number of these—and the number of distorted cells is astronomical —resemble fertilized ova. Some of them resemble them so closely that I personally would not enjoy the task of distinguishing between them and the real thing. However, the body as a whole is not that particular; anything which even roughly resembles a fertilized egg-cell is capable of commanding that counterplacenta.

"Now consider the source of these cells—physiologically speaking, gland tissue—a mass of capillary tubes and blood vessels. Each and every one of these does its best to accept and nurture these fetal imitations, down to the tiniest of them. The thin walls of the capillaries, however, break down easily under such an effort, and the imitations—selectively, the best of them, too, because the tissues yield most readily to them—they pass into the capillaries and then into the bloodstream.

"There is one place and only one place where they can be combed out; and it's a place rich in oxygen, lymph, blood and plasma: the lungs. The lungs enthusiastically take on the job of forming placentae for these cells, and nurturing them. But for every segment of lung given over to gestating an imitation fetus, there is one less segment occupied with the job of oxygenating blood. Ultimately the lungs fail, and death results from oxygen starvation."

Rathburn spoke up. "For years chorio was regarded as a lung disease, and the cancerous gonads as a sort of side effect."

"But lung cancer—" Keogh began to object.

"It isn't lung cancer, don't you see? Given enough time, it might be, through metastasis. But there is never enough time. Chorio doesn't have to wait for that, to kill. That's why it's so swift." He tried not to look at the girl, and failed; he said it anyway: "And certain."

"Just exactly how do you treat it?"

Weber raised his hands and let them fall. It was precisely the gesture Rathburn had made earlier, and Keogh wondered distantly whether they taught it in medical schools. "Something to kill the pain. Orchidectomy might make the patient last a little longer, by removing the supply of wild cells to the bloodstream. But it wouldn't save him. Metastasis has already taken place by the time the first symptom appears. The cancer becomes generalized . . . perhaps the lung condition is only God's mercy."

"What's 'orchidectomy'?" asked Keogh.

"Amputation of the—uh—source," said Rathburn uncomfortably.

"No!" cried the girl.

Keogh sent her a pitying look. There was that about

him which was cynical, sophisticated, and perhaps coldly angry at anyone who lived as he could never live, had what he could never have. It was a stirring of the grave ancient sin which old Cap'n Gamaliel had isolated in his perspicacious thoughts. Sure, amputate, if it'll help, he thought. What do you think you're preserving—his virility? What good's it to you now? . . . but sending her the look, he encountered something different from the romantically based horror and shock he expected. Her thick level brows were drawn together, her whole face intense with taut concentration. "Let me think," she said, oddly.

"You really should—" Rathburn began, but she shushed him with any impatient gesture. The three men exchanged a glance and settled back; it was as if someone, something had told them clearly and specifically to wait. What they were waiting for, they could not imagine.

The girl sat with her eyes closed. A minute crawled by. "Daddy used to say," she said, so quietly that she must surely be talking to herself, "that there's always a way. All you have to do is think of it."

There was another long silence and she opened her eyes. There was a burning down in them somewhere; it made Keogh uneasy. She said, "And once he told me that I could have anything I wanted; all it had to be was . . . possible. And . . . the only way you can find out if a thing is impossible is to try it."

"That wasn't Sam Wyke," said Keogh. "That was Keogh."

She wet her lips and looked at them each in turn. She seemed not to see them at all. "I'm not going to let him die," she said. "You'll see."

Sammy Stein came back two years later, on leave, and full of plans to join the Army Air Force. He'd had, as he himself said, the hell kicked out of him in China and a lot of the hellishness as well. But there was enough of the old Sammy left to make wild wonderful plans about going trespassing; and they knew just where they were going. The new Sammy, however, demanded a binge and a broad first.

Guy, two years out of high school, working for a living, and by nature neither binger nor wencher, went along only too gladly. Sam seemed to have forgotten about the "ol' swimmin' hole" at first, and halfway through the evening, in a local bar-and-dance emporium, Guy was about to despair of his ever remembering it, when Sam himself brought it up, recalling to Guy that he had once written Sam a letter asking Sam if it had really happened. Guy had, in his turn, forgotten the letter, and after that they had a good time with "remember-when"—and they made plans to go trespassing the very next day, and bring a lunch. And start early.

Then there was a noisy involvement with some girls, and a lot more drinks, and out of the haze and movement somewhere after midnight, Guy emerged on a sidewalk looking at Sammy shoveling a girl into a taxicab. "Hey!" he called out, "what about the you know, ol' swimmin' hole?"

"Call me Abacus, you can count on me," said Sammy, and laughed immoderately. The girl with him pulled at his arm; he shook her off and weaved over to Guy. "Listen," he said, and gave a distorted wink, "if this makes—and it will—I'm starting no early starts. Tell you what, you go on out there and meet me by that sign says keep out or we'll castigate you. Say eleven o'clock. If I can't make it by then I'm dead or something." He bellowed at the cab, "You gon' kill me, honey?" and the girl called back, "I will if you don't get into this taxi." "See what I mean?" said Sammy in a grand drunken nonsequitur, "I got to go get killed." He zigged away, needing no zag because even walking sidewise he reached the cab in a straight line, and Guy saw no more of him that leave.

That was hard to take, mostly because there was no

special moment at which he knew Sammy wasn't coming. He arrived ten minutes late, after making a super-human effort to get there. His stomach was sour from the unaccustomed drinking, and he was sandy-eyed and ache-jointed from lack of sleep. He knew that the greater probability was that Sammy had not arrived yet or would not at all; yet the nagging possibility existed that he had come early and gone straight in. Guy waited around for a full hour, and some more minutes until the little road was clear of traffic and sounds of traffic, and then plunged alone into the woods, past the No Trespassing sign, and in to the wall. He had trouble finding the two trees, and once over the wall, he could not get his bearings for a while; he was pleased, of course, to find the unbelievably perfect lawns still there by the flawless acre, the rigidly controlled museums of carven box, the edge-trimmed, rolled-gravel walks meandering prettily through the woods. The pleasure, however, was no more than confirmation of his memory, and went no further; the day was spoiled.

Guy reached the lake at nearly one o'clock, hot, tired, ravenously hungry and unpleasantly nervous. The combination hit him in the stomach and made it echo; he sat down on the bank and ate. He wolfed down the food he had brought for himself and Sammy's as well—odds and ends carelessly tossed into a paper sack in the bleary early hours. The cake was moldy but he ate it anyway. The orange juice was warm and had begun to ferment. And stubbornly, he determined to swim, because that was what he had come for.

He chose the beach with the golden sand. Under a thick cover of junipers he found a stone bench and table. He undressed here and scuttled across the beach and into the water.

He had meant it to be a mere dip, so he could say he'd done it. But around the little headland to the left was the rectangular cove with the diving platform; and he remembered the harbor of model ships; and then movement diagonally across the foot of the lake's L caught his eye, and he saw models—not the anchored ships this time, but racing sloops, which put out from an inlet and crossed its mouth and sailed in again; they must be mounted on some sort of underwater wheel or endless chain, and moved as the breeze took them. He all but boiled straight across to them, then decided to be wise and go round.

He swam to the left and the rocky shore, and worked his way along it. Clinging close (the water seemed bottomless here) he rounded the point and came face to face (literally; they touched) with a girl.

She was young—near his age—and his first impression was of eyes of too complex an architecture, blue-white teeth with pointed canines quite unlike the piano-key regularity considered beautiful in these times, and a wide cape of rich brown hair afloat around her shoulders. By then his gasp was completed, and in view of the fact that in gasping he had neglected to remove his mouth from the water, he was shut off from outside impressions for a strangling time, until he felt a firm grasp on his left biceps and found himself returned to the side of the rock.

"Th-thanks," he said hoarsely as she swam back a yard and trod water. "I'm not supposed to be here," he added inanely.

"I guess I'm not either. But I thought you lived here. I thought you were a faun."

"Boy am I glad to hear that. I mean about you. All I am is a trespasser. Boy."

"I'm not a boy."

"It was just a finger of speech," he said, using one of the silly expressions which come to a person as he grows, and blessedly pass. She seemed not to react to it at all, for she said gravely, "You have the most beautiful eyes I have ever seen. They are made of aluminum. And your hair is all wiggly."

He could think of nothing to say to that, but tried; all that emerged was, "We'll, it's early yet," and suddenly they were laughing together. She was so strange, so different. She spoke in a grave, unaccented, and utterly incautious idiom as if she thought strange thoughts and spoke them right out. "Also," she said, "you have lovely lips. They're pale blue. You ought to get out of the water."

"I can't!"

She considered that for a moment, treading away from him and then back to the yard's distance. "Where are your things?"

He pointed across the narrow neck of the lake which he had circumnavigated.

"Wait for me over there," she said, and suddenly swam close, so close she could dip her chin and look straight into his eyes. "You got to," she said fiercely.

"Oh I will," he promised, and struck out for the opposite shore. She hung to the rock, watching him.

Swimming, reaching hard, stretching for distance warmed him, and the chill and its accompanying vague ache diminished. Then he had a twinge of stomach-ache, and he drew up his knees to ease it. When he tried to extend himself again, he could, but it hurt too much. He drew up his knees again, and the pain followed inward so that to flex again was out of the question. He drew his knees up still tighter, and tighter still followed the pain. He needed air badly by then, threw up his head, tried to roll over on his back; but with his knees drawn up, everything came out all wrong. He inhaled at last because he had to, but the air was gone away somewhere; he floundered upward for it until the pressure in his ears told him he was swimming downward. Blackness came upon him and receded, and came again, he let it come for a tired instant, and was surrounded by light, and drew one lungful of air and one of water, and got the blackness again; this time it stayed with him . . .

Still beautiful in her bed, but morphine-clouded, fly-papered, and unstruggling in viscous sleep, he lay with monsters swarming in his veins . . .

Quietly, in a corner of the room, she spoke with Keogh:

"You don't understand me. You didn't understand me yesterday when I cried out at the idea of that—that operation. Keogh, I love him, but I'm *me*. Loving him doesn't mean I've stopped thinking. Loving him means I'm more me than ever, not less. It means I can do anything I did before, only more, only better. That's why I fell in love with him. That's why I am in love with him. Weren't you ever in love, Keogh?"

He looked at the way her hair fell, and the earnest placement of her thick soft brows, and he said, "I haven't thought much about it."

"There's always a way. All you have to do is think of it," she quoted. "Keogh, I've accepted what Dr. Rathburn said. After I left you yesterday I went to the library and tore the heart out of some books . . . they're right, Rathburn and Weber. And I've thought and I've thought . . . trying the way Daddy would, to turn everything upside down and backwards, to look for a new way of thinking. He won't die, Keogh; I'm not going to let him die."

"You said you accepted—"

"Oh, part of him. Most of him, if you like. We all die, bit by bit, all the time, and it doesn't bother us because most of the dead parts are replaced. He'll . . . he'll lose more parts, sooner, but—after it's over, he'll be himself again." She said it with superb confidence—perhaps it was childlike. If so, it was definitely not childish.

"You have an idea," said Keogh positively. As he had pointed out to the doctors, he knew her.

"All those—those things in his blood," she said quietly. "The struggle they go through . . . they're trying to survive; did you ever think of it that way, Keogh? They want to live. They want most terribly to go on living."

"I hadn't thought about it."

"His body wants them to live too. It welcomes them wherever they lodge. Dr. Weber said so."

"You've got hold of something," said Keogh flatly, "and whatever it is I don't think I like it."

"I don't want you to like it," she said in the same strange quiet voice. He looked swiftly at her and saw again the burning deep in her eyes. He had to look away. She said, "I want you to hate it. I want you to fight it. You have one of the most wonderful minds I have ever known, Keogh, and I want you to think up every argument you can think of against it. For every argument I'll find an answer, and then we'll know what to do."

"You'd better go ahead," he said reluctantly.

"I had a pretty bad quarrel with Dr. Weber this morning," she said suddenly.

"This m—when?" He looked at his watch; it was still early.

"About three, maybe four. In his room. I went there and woke him up."

"Look, you don't do things like that to Weber!"

"I do. Anyway, he's gone."

He rose to his feet, the rare bright patches of anger showing in his cheeks. He took a breath, let it out, and sat down again. "You'd better tell me about it."

"In the library," she said, "there's a book on genetics, and it mentions some experiments on Belgian hares. The does were impregnated without sperm, with some sort of saline or alkaline solution."

"I remember something about it." He was well used to her circuitous way of approaching something important. She built conversational points, not like a hired contractor, but like an architect. Sometimes she brought in portions of her lumber and stacked them beside the structure. If she ever did that, it was material she needed and would use. He waited.

"The does gave birth to baby rabbits, all female. The interesting thing was that they were identical to each other and to the mother. Even the blood-vessel patterns in the eyeball were so similar that an expert might be fooled by photographs of them. 'Impossibly similar' is what one of the experimenters called it. They had to be identical because everything they inherited was from the mother. I woke Dr. Weber up to tell him about that."

"And he told you he'd read the book."

"He wrote it," she said gently. "And then I told him that if he could do that with a Belgian hare, he could do it with"—she nodded toward her big bed—"him."

Then she was quiet, while Keogh rejected the idea, found it stuck to his mind's hand, not to be shaken off; brought it to his mind's eye and shuddered away from it, shook again and failed, slowly brought it close and turned it over, and turned it again.

"Take one of those—those things like fertilized ova—make it grow . . ."

"You don't *make* it grow. It wants desperately to grow. And not one of them, Keogh. You have thousands. You have hundreds more every hour."

"Oh my God."

"It came to me when Dr. Rathbun suggested the operation. It came to me all at once, a miracle. If you love someone that much," she said, looking at the sleeper, "miracles happen. But you have to be willing to help them happen." She looked at him directly, with an intensity that made him move back in his chair. "I can have anything I want—all it has to be is possible. We just have to make it possible. That's why I went to Dr. Weber this morning. To ask him."

"He said it wasn't possible."

"He said that at first. After a half hour or so he said the odds against it were in the billions or trillions . . .

but you see, as soon as he said that, he was saying it was possible."

"What did you do then?"

"I dared him to try."

"And that's why he left?"

"Yes."

"You're mad," he said before he could stop himself. She seemed not to resent it. She sat calmly, waiting.

"Look," said Keogh at last, "Weber said those distorted —uh—*things* were *like* fertilized ova. He never said they were. He could have said—well, I'll say it for him— they're *not* fertilized ova."

"But he did say they were—some of them, anyway, and especially those that reached the lungs—were very much like ova. How close do you have to get before there's no real difference at all?"

"It can't be. It just can't."

"Weber said that. And I asked him if he had ever tried."

"All right, all right! It can't happen, but just to keep this silly argument going, suppose you got something that would grow. You won't, of course. But if you did, how would you keep it growing. It has to be fed, it has to be kept at a certain critical temperature, a certain amount of acid or alkali will kill it . . . you don't just plant something like that in the yard."

"Already they've taken ova from one cow, planted them in another, and gotten calves. There's a man in Australia who plans to raise blooded cattle from scrub cows that way."

"You *have* done your homework."

"Oh, that isn't all. There's a Dr. Carrel in New Jersey who has been able to keep chicken tissue alive for months —he says indefinitely—in a nutrient solution, in a temperature-controlled jar in his lab. It grows, Keogh! It grows so much he has to cut it away every once in a while."

"This is crazy. This is—it's insane," he growled. "And what do you think you'll get if you bring one of these monsters to term?"

"We'll bring thousands of them to term," she said composedly. "And one of them will be—*him*." She leaned forward abruptly, and her even tone of voice broke; a wildness grew through her face and voice, and though it was quiet, it shattered him: "It will be his flesh, the pattern of him, his own substance grown again. His hair, Keogh. His fingerprints. His—eyes. His—his *self*."

"I can't—" Keogh shook himself like a wet spaniel, but it changed nothing; he was still here, she, the bed, the sleeper, and this dreadful, this inconceivably horrible, wrong idea.

She smiled then, put out her hand and touched him; incredibly, it was a mother's smile, warm and comforting, a mother's loving, protective touch; her voice was full of affection. "Keogh, if it won't work, it won't work, no matter what we do. Then you'll be right. I think it will work. It's what I want. Don't you want me to have what I want?"

He had to smile, and she smiled back. "You're a young devil," he said ardently. "Got me coming and going, haven't you? Why did you want me to fight it?"

"I didn't," she said, "but if you fight me, you'll come up with problems nobody else could possibly think of, and once we've thought of them, we'll be ready, don't you see? I'll fight with you, Keogh," she said, shifting her strange bright spectrum from tenderness to a quiet, convinced, invincible certainty. "I'll fight with you, I'll lift and carry, I'll buy and sell and kill if I have to, but I am going to bring him back. You know something, Keogh?"

She waved her hand in a gesture that included him, the room, the castle and grounds and all the other castle and grounds; the pseudonyms, the ships and trains, the factories and exchanges, the mountains and acres and mines and banks and the thousands of people which, taken together, were Wyke: "I always knew that all this *was*," she said, "and I've come to understand that this is mine. But I used to wonder sometimes, what it was all *for*. Now I know. Now I know."

A mouth on his mouth, a weight on his stomach. He felt boneless and nauseated, limp as grease drooling. The light around him was green, and all shapes blurred.

The mouth on his mouth, the weight on his stomach, a breath of air, welcome but too warmm, too moist. He needed it desperately but did not like it, and found a power-plant full of energy to gather it up in his lungs and fling it away; but his weakness so filtered all that effort that it emerged in a faint bubbling sigh.

The mouth on his mouth again, and the weight on his stomach and another breath. He tried to turn his head but someone held him by the nose. He blew out the needed, unsatisfactory air and replaced it by a little gust of his own inhalation. On this he coughed; it was too rich, pure, too good. He coughed as one does over a pickle-barrel; good air hurt his lungs.

He felt his head and shoulders lifted, shifted, by which he learned that he had been flat on his back on stone, or something flat and quite that hard, and was now on smooth, firm softness. The good sharp air came and went, his weak coughs fewer, until he fell into a dazed peace. The face that bent over his was too close to focus, or he had lost the power to focus; either way, he didn't care. Drowsily he stared up into the blurred brightness of that face and listened uncritically to the voice—

—the voice crooning wordlessly and comfortingly, and somehow, in its wordlessness, creating new expressions for joy and delight for which words would not do. Then after all there were words, half sung, half whispered; and he couldn't catch them, and he couldn't catch them and then . . . and then he was sure he heard: "How could it be, such a magic as this: all this and the eyes as well . . . " Then, demanding, "You are the shape of the not-you: tell me, are *you* in there?"

He opened his eyes wide and saw her face clearly at last and the dark hair, and the eyes were green—true deep sea-green. Her tangled hair, drying, crowned her like vines, and the leafy roof close above seemed part of her and the green eyes, and threw green light on the unaccountably blond transparency of her cheeks. He genuinely did not know, at the moment, what she was. She had said to him (was it years ago?) "I thought you were a faun . . ." he had not, at the moment, much consciousness, not to say whimsy, at his command; she was simply something unrelated to anything in his experience.

He was aware of griping, twisting pain rising, filling, about to explode in his upper abdomen. Some thick wire within him had kinked, and knowing well that it should be unbent, he made a furious, rebellious effort and pulled it through. The explosion came, but in nausea, not in agony. Convulsively he turned his head, surged upward, and let it go.

He saw with too much misery to be horrified the bright vomit surging on and around her knee, and running into the crevice between thigh and calf where she had her leg bent and tucked under her, and the clots left there as the fluid ran away. And she—

She sat where she was, held his head, cradled him in her arms, soothed him and crooned to him and said that was good, good; he'd feel better now. The weakness floored him and receded; then shakily he pressed away from her, sat up, bowed his head and gasped for breath. "Whooo," he said.

"Boy," she said; and she said it in exact concert with him. He clung to his shins and wiped the nausea-tears from his left eye, then his right, on his knee-cap. "Boy oh boy," he said, and she said it with him in concert.

So at last he looked at her.

He looked at her, and would never forget what he saw, and exactly the way it was. Late sunlight made into lace by the bower above clothed her; she leaned toward him, one small hand flat on the ground, one slim supporting arm straight and straight down; her weight turned up that shoulder and her head tilted toward it as if drawn down by the heavy darkness of her hair. It gave a sense of yielding, as if she were fragile, which he knew she was not. Her other hand lay open across one knee, the palm up and the fingers not quite relaxed, as if they held something; and indeed they did, for a spot of light, gold turned coral by her flesh, lay in her palm. She held it just so, just right, unconsciously, and her hand held that rare knowledge that closed, a hand may not give nor receive. For his lifetime he had it all, each tiniest part, even to the gleaming big toenail at the underside of her other calf. And she was smiling, and her complex eyes adored.

Guy Gibbon knew his life's biggest moment during the moment itself, a rarity in itself, and of all times of life, it was time to say the unforgettable, for anything he said now would be.

He shuddered, and then smiled back at her. "Oh . . . boy," he breathed.

And again they were laughing together until, puzzled, he stopped and asked, "Where am I?"

She would not answer, so he closed his eyes and puzzled it out. Pine bower . . . undress somewhere . . . swimming. Oh, swimming. And then across the lake, and he had met— He opened his eyes and looked at her and said, "You." Then swimming back, cold, his gut full of too much food and warm juice and moldy cake to boot, and, ". . . you must have saved my life."

"Well somebody had to. You were dead."

"I should've been."

"No!" she cried. "Don't you ever say that again!" And he could see she was absolutely serious.

"I only meant, for stupidity. I ate a lot of junk, and some cake I think was moldy. Too much, when I was hot and tired, and then like a bonehead I went right into the water, so anybody who does that deserves to—"

"I meant it," she said levelly, "never again. Didn't you ever hear of the old tradition of the field of battle, when one man saved another's life, that life became his to do what he wanted with?"

"What do you want to do with mine?"

"That depends," she said thoughtfully. "You have to give it. I can't just take it." She knelt then and sat back on her heels, her hands trailing pine-needles across the bower's paved stone floor. She bowed her head and her hair swung forward. He thought she was watching him through it; he could not be sure.

He said, and the thought grew so large that it quelled his voice and made him whisper. "Do you want it?"

"Oh, yes," she said, whispering too. When he moved to her and put her hair back to see if she was watching him, he found her eyes closed, and tears pressed through. He reached for her gently, but before he could touch her she sprang up and straight at the leafy wall. Her long golden body passed through it without a sound, and seemed to hang suspended outside; then it was gone. He put his head through and saw her flashing along under green water. He hesitated, then got an acrid whiff of his own vomit. The water looked clean and the golden sand just what he ached to scrub himself with. He climbed out of the bower and floundered clumsily down the bank and into the water.

After his first plunge he came up and spun about, looking for her, but she was gone.

Numbly he swam to the tiny beach and, kneeling, scoured himself with the fine sand. He dove and rinsed, and then (hoping) scrubbed himself all over again. And rinsed. But he did not see her.

He stood in the late rays of the sun to dry, and looked off across the lake. His heart leapt when he saw white movement, and sank again as he saw it was just the wheel of boats bobbing and sliding there.

He plodded up to the bower—now at last he saw it was the one behind which he had undressed—and he sank down on the bench.

This was a place where tropical fish swam in ocean water where there was no ocean, and where fleets of tiny perfect boats sailed with no one sailing them and no one watching, and where priceless statues stood hidden in clipped and barbered glades deep in the woods and—and he hadn't seen it all; what other impossibilities were possible in this impossible place?

And besides, he'd been sick. (He wrinkled his nostrils.) Damn near . . . drowned. Out of his head for sure, for a while anyway. She couldn't be real. Hadn't he noticed a greenish cast to her flesh, or was that just the light? . . . anybody who could make a place like this, run a place like this, could jimmy up some kind of machine to hypnotize you like in the science fiction stories.

He stirred uneasily. Maybe someone was watching him, even now.

Hurriedly, he began to dress.

So she wasn't real. Or maybe all of it wasn't real. He'd bumped into that other trespasser across the lake there, and that was real, but then when he'd almost drowned, he'd dreamed up the rest.

Only—he touched his mouth. He'd dreamed up someone blowing the breath back into him. He'd heard about that somewhere, but it sure wasn't what they were teaching this year at the Y.

You are the shape of the not-you. Are you in there?
What did that mean?

He finished dressing dazedly. He muttered, "What'd I hafta go an' eat that goddam cake for?" He wondered what he would tell Sammy. If she wasn't real, Sammy wouldn't know what he was talking about. If she was real there's only one thing he would talk about, yes, and from then on. You mean you had her in that place and all you did was throw up on her? No—he wouldn't tell Sammy. Or anybody.

And he'd be a bachelor all his life.

Boy oh boy. What an introduction. First she has to save your life and then you don't know what to say and then oh, look what you had to go and do. But anyway—she wasn't real.

He wondered what her name was. Even if she wasn't real. Lots of people don't use their real names.

He climbed out of the bower and crossed the silent pine carpet behind it, and he shouted. It was not a word at all, and had nothing about it that tried to make it one.

She was standing there waiting for him. She wore a quiet brown dress and low heels and carried a brown leather pocketbook, and her hair was braided and tied neatly and sedately in a coronet. She looked, too, as if she had turned down some inward tone control so that her skin did not radiate. She looked ready to disappear, not into thin air, but into a crowd—any crowd, as soon as she could get close to one. In a crowd he would have walked right past her, certainly, but for the shape of her eyes. She stepped up to him quickly and laid her hand on his cheek and laughed up at him. Again he saw the whiteness of those unusual eyeteeth, so sharp . . .

No blusher in history was ever stopped by that observation. He asked, "Which way do you go?"

She looked at his eyes, one, the other, both, quickly; then folded her long hands together around the strap of her pocketbook and looked down at them.

"With you," she said softly.

This was only one of the many things she said to him, moment by moment, which gained meaning for him as time went on. He took her back to town and to dinner, and then to the West Side address she gave him and they stood outside it all night talking. In six weeks they were married.

"How could I argue," said Weber to Dr. Rathburn.

They stood together watching a small army of workmen swarming over the gigantic stone barn a quarter-mile from the castle, which, incidentally, was invisible from this point and unknown to the men. Work had begun at three the previous afternoon, continued all night. There was nothing, nothing at all that Dr. Weber had specified which was not only given him, but on the site or already installed.

"I know," said Rathburn, who did.

"Not only, how could I argue," said Weber, "why should I? A man has plans, ambitions. That Keogh, what an approach! That's the first thing he went after—my plans for myself. That's where he starts. And suddenly everything you ever wanted to do or be or have is handed to you or promised to you, and no fooling about the promise either."

"*Oh* no. They don't need to fool anybody . . . You want to pass a prognosis?"

"You mean on the youngster there?" He looked at Rathburn. "Oh—that's not what you mean . . . You're asking me if I can bring one of those surrogate fetuses to term. An opinion like that would make a damn fool out of a man, and this is no job for a damn fool. All I can tell you is, I tried it—and that is something I wouldn't't've dreamed of doing if it hadn't been for her and her crazy idea. I left here at four A.M. with some throat smears and by nine I had a half dozen of them isolated and in nutrient solution. Beef blood plasma—the quickest thing I could get ready. And I got mitosis. They divided, and in a few

hours I could see two of 'em dimpling to form the gastro-
sphere. That was evidence enough to get going; that's all
I think and that's all I told them on the phone. And by
the time I got here," he added, waving toward the big
barn, "there's a research lab four fifths built, big enough
for a city medical center. Argue?" he demanded, return-
ing to Dr. Rathburn's original question. "How could I
argue? Why should I? . . . And that *girl*. She's a force, like
gravity. She can turn on so much pressure, and I mean by
herself and personally, that she could probably get anything in the world she wanted even if she didn't own it,
the world I mean. Put that in the northeast entrance!" he
bellowed at a foreman. "I'll be down to show you just
where it goes." He turned to Rathburn; he was a man on
fire. "I got to go."

"Anything I can do," said Dr. Rathburn, "just say it."

"That's the wonderful part of it," said Weber. "That's
what everybody around here keeps saying, and they mean
it!" He trotted down toward the barn, and Rathburn
turned toward the castle.

About a month after his last venture at trespassing, Guy
Gibbon was coming home from work when a man at the
corner put away a newspaper and, still folding it, said,
"Gibbon?"

"That's right," said Guy, a little sharply.

The man looked him up and down, quickly, but giving
an impression of such thoroughness, efficiency, and experience that Guy would not have been surprised to learn
that the man had not only catalogued his clothes and their
source, their state of maintenance and a computation
therefrom of his personal habits, but also his state of
health and even his blood type. "My name's Keogh," said
the man. "Does that mean anything to you?"

"No."

"Sylva never mentioned the name?"

"Sylva! N-no, she didn't."

"Let's go somewhere and have a drink. I'd like to talk to you." Something had pleased this man: Guy wondered what. "Well, okay," he said. "Only I don't drink much, but well, okay."

They found a bar in the neighborhood with booths in the back. Keogh had a Scotch and soda and Guy, after some hesitation, ordered beer. Guy said, "You know her?"

"Most of her life. Do you?"

"What? Well, sure. We're going to get married." He looked studiously into his beer and said uncomfortably, "What are you anyway, Mr. Keogh?"

"You might say," said Keogh, "I'm *in loco parentis.*" He waited for a response, then added, "Sort of a guardian."

"She never said anything about a guardian."

"I can understand that. What has she told you about herself?"

Guy's discomfort descended to a level of shyness, diffidence, even a touch of fear—which did not alter the firmness of his words, however they were spoken. "I don't know you, Mr. Keogh. I don't think I ought to answer any questions about Sylva. Or me. Or anything." He looked up at the man. Keogh searched deeply, then smiled. It was an unpracticed and apparently slightly painful process with him, but was genuine for all that. "Good!" he barked, and rose. "Come on." He left the booth and Guy, more than a little startled, followed. They went to the phone booth in the corner. Keogh dropped in a nickel, dialed, and waited, his eyes fixed on Guy. Then Guy had to listen to one side of the conversation:

"I'm here with Guy Gibbon." (Guy had to notice that Keogh identified himself only with his voice.)

...."Of course I knew about it. That's a silly question, girl."

...."Because it *is* my business. *You* are my business."

. . ."Stop it? I'm not trying to stop anything. I just have to know, that's all."

. . ."All right. All right . . . He's here. He won't talk about you or anything, which is good. Yes, very good. Will you please tell him to open up?"

And he handed the receiver to a startled Guy, who said tremulously, "Uh, hello," to it while watching Keogh's impassive face.

Her voice suffused and flooded him, changed this whole unsettling experience to something different and good. "Guy, darling."

"Sylva—"

"It's all right. I should have told you sooner, I guess. It had to come some time. Guy, you can tell Keogh anything you like. Anything he asks."

"Why, honey? Who is he, anyway?"

There was a pause, then a strange little laugh. "He can explain that better than I can. You want us to be married, Guy?"

"Oh yes!"

"Well all right then. Nobody can change that, nobody but you. And listen, Guy. I'll live anywhere, any way you want to live. That's the real truth and all of it, do you believe me?"

"I always believe you."

"All right then. So that's what we'll do. Now you go and talk to Keogh. Tell him anything he wants to know. He has to do the same. I love you, Guy."

"Me too," said Guy, watching Keogh's face. "Well, okay then," he added when she said nothing further. " 'Bye." He hung up and he and Keogh had a long talk.

"It hurts him," she whispered to Dr. Rathburn.

"I know." He shook his head sympathetically. "There's just so much morphine you can ram into a man, though."

"Just a little more?"

"Maybe a little," he said sadly. He went to his bag and got the needle. Sylva kissed the sleeping man tenderly and left the room. Keogh was waiting for her.

He said, "This has got to stop, girl."

"Why?" she responded ominously.

"Let's get out of here."

She had known Keogh so long, and so well, that she was sure he had no surprises for her. But this voice, this look, these were something new in Keogh. He held the door for her, so she preceded him through it and then went where he silently led.

They left the castle and took the path through a heavy copse and over the brow of the hill which overlooked the barn. The parking lot, which had once been a barnyard, was full of automobiles. A white ambulance approached; another was unloading at the northeast platform. A muffled generator purred somewhere behind the building, and smoke rose from the stack of the new stone boiler room at the side. They both looked avidly at the building but did not comment. The path took them along the crest of the hill and down toward the lake. They went to a small forest clearing in which stood an eight-foot Diana, the huntress Diana, chaste and fleet-footed, so beautifully finished she seemed not like marble at all, not like anything cold or static. "I always had the idea," said Keogh, "that nobody can lie anywhere near her."

She looked up at the Diana.

"Not even to themselves," said Keogh, and plumped down on a marble bench.

"Let's have it," she said.

"You want to make Guy Gibbon happen all over again. It's a crazy idea and it's a big one too. But lots of things were crazier, and some bigger, and now they're commonplace. I won't argue on how crazy it is, or how big."

"What then?"

"I've been trying, the last day or so, to back 'way out,

far off, get a look at this thing with some perspective. Sylva, you've forgotten something."

"Good," she said. "Oh, good. I knew you'd think of things like this before it was too late."

"So you can find a way out?" Slowly he shook his head. "Not this time. Tighten up the Wyke guts, girl, and make up your mind to quit."

"Go ahead."

"It's just this. I don't believe you're going to get your carbon copy, mind you, but you just might. I've been talking to Weber, and by God you just about might. But if you do, all you've got is a container, and nothing to fill it with. Look, girl, a man isn't blood and bone and body cells, and that's all."

He paused, until she said, "Go on, Keogh."

He demanded, "You love this guy?"

"Keogh!" She was amused.

"Whaddaya love?" he barked. "That skrinkly hair? The muscles, skin? His nat'ral equipment? The eyes, voice?"

"All that," she said composedly.

"All that, and that's all?" he demanded relentlessly. "Because if your answer is yes, you can have what you want, and more power to you, and good riddance. I don't know anything about love, but I will say this: that if that's all there is to it, the hell with it."

"Well of *course* there's more."

"Ah. And where are you going to get that, girl? Listen, a man is skin and bone he stands in, plus what's in his head, plus what's in his heart. You mean to reproduce Guy Gibbon, but you're not going to do it by duplicating his carcass. You want to duplicate the whole man, you're going to have to make him live the same life again. And that you can't do."

She looked up at the Diana for a long time. Then, "Why not?" she breathed.

"I'll tell you why not," he said angrily. "Because first of all you have to find out *who he is*."

"I know who he is!"

He spat explosively on the green moss by the bench. It was totally uncharacteristic and truly shocking. "You don't know a particle, and I know even less. I had his back against a wall one time for better than two hours, trying to find out who he is. He's just another kid, is all. Nothing much in school, nothing much at sports, same general tastes and feelings as six zillion other ones like him. Why him, Sylva? Why him? What did you ever see in a guy like that to be worth the marrying?"

"I . . . didn't know you disliked him."

"Oh hell, girl, I don't! I never said that. I can't—I can't even find anything to dislike."

"You don't know him the way I do."

"There, I agree. I don't and I couldn't. Because you don't know anything either—you *feel*, but you don't *know*. If you want to see Guy Gibbon again, or a reasonable facsimile, he's going to have to live by a script from the day he's born. He'll have to duplicate every experience that this kid here ever had."

"All right," she said quietly.

He looked at her, stunned. He said, "And before he can do that, we have to write the script. And before we can write it, we have to get the material somehow. What do you expect to do—set up a foundation or something dedicated to the discovery of each and every moment this—this unnoticeable young man ever lived through? And do it secretly, because while he's growing up he can't ever know? Do you know how much that would cost, how many people it would involve?"

"That would be all right," she said.

"And suppose you had it, a biography written like a script, twenty years of a lifetime, every day, every hour you could account for; now you're going to have to arrange for a child, from birth, to be surrounded by people who are going to play this script out—and who will never let anything else happen to him but what's in the script, and who will never let him know."

"That's it! That's it!" she cried.

He leapt to his feet and swore at her. He said, "I'm not planning this, you lovestruck lunatic, I'm objecting to it!"

"Is there any more?" she cried eagerly. "Keogh, Keogh, try—try hard. How do we start? What do we do first? Quick, Keogh."

He looked at her, thunderstruck, and at last sank down on the bench and began to laugh weakly. She sat by him, held his hand, her eyes shining. After a time he sobered, and turned to her. He drank the shine of those eyes for a while; and after, his brain began to function again . . . on Wyke business . . .

"The main source of who he is and what he's done," he said at last, "won't be with us much longer . . . We better go tell Rathburn to get him off the morphine. He has to be able to think."

"All right," she said. "All right."

When the pain got too much to permit him to remember any more, they tried a little morphine again. For a while they found a balance between recollection and agony, but the agony gained. Then they severed his spinal cord so he couldn't feel it. They brought in people— psychiatrist, stenographers, even a professional historian.

In the rebuilt barn, Weber tried animal hosts, cows even, and primates—everything he could think of. He got some results, though no good ones. He tried humans too. He couldn't cross the bridge of body tolerance; the uterus will not support an alien fetus any more than the hand will accept the graft of another's finger.

So he tried nutrient solutions. He tried a great many.

Ultimately he found one that worked. It was the blood plasma of pregnant women.

He placed the best of the quasiova between sheets of sterilized chamois. He designd automatic machinery to drip the plasma in at arterial tempo, drain it at a veinous rate, keep it at body temperature.

One day fifty of them died, because of the chloroform used in one of the adhesives. When light seemed to affect them adversely, Weber designed containers of bakelite. When ordinary photography proved impractical, he designed a new kind of film sensitive to heat, the first infrared film.

The viable fetuses he had at sixty days showed the eye-spot, the spine, the buds of arms, a beating heart. Each and every one of them consumed, or was bathed in, over a gallon of plasma a day, and at one point there were one hundred and seventy-four thousand of them. Then they began to die off—some malformed, some chemically unbalanced, many for reasons too subtle even for Weber and his staff.

When he had done all he could, when he could only wait and see, he had fetuses seven months along and growing well. There were twenty-three of them. Guy Gibbon was dead quite a while by then, and his widow came to see Weber and tiredly put down a stack of papers and reports, urged him to read, begged him to call her as soon as he had.

He read them, he called her. He refused what she asked.

She got hold of Keogh. He refused to have anything to do with such an idea. She made him change his mind. Keogh made Weber change his mind.

The stone barn hummed with construction again, and new machinery. The cold tank was four by six feet inside,

surrounded by coils and sensing devices. They put her
in it.

By that time the fetuses were eight and a half months
along. There were four left.

One made it.

Author's note: To the reader, but especially to the reader
in his early twenties, let me ask: did you ever have the
feeling that you were getting pushed around? Did you
ever want to do something, and have all sorts of obstacles
thrown in your way until you had to give up, while on
the other hand some other thing you wanted was made
easy for you? Did you ever feel that certain strangers
know who you are? Did you ever meet a girl who made
you explode inside, who seemed to like you—and who
was mysteriously plucked out of your life, as if she
shouldn't be in the script?

Well, we've all had these feelings. Yet if you've read
the above, you'll allow it's a little more startling than just
a story. It reads like an analogy, doesn't it? I mean, it
doesn't have to be a castle, or the ol' swimmin' hole, and
the names have been changed to protect the innocent . . .
author.

Because it could be about time for her to wake up, aged
only two or three years for her twenty-year cold sleep.
And when she meets you, it's going to be the biggest thing
that ever happened to you since the last time.